THE TRUTH ABOUT THE LADY

WHISPERS OF THE TON (BOOK 6)

ROSE PEARSON

THE TRUTH ABOUT THE LADY

PROLOGUE

"This year, you must be *different*!"

Hyacinth swallowed hard and dropped her head. There was no response she could give, nothing that she could say that would appease her ferocious mother.

"You have already ruined your reputation by hiding away," Lady Coatbridge continued, walking up and down the drawing room, gesturing at Hyacinth now and again. "Last Season was your come out and what did you do?"

Hyacinth winced, though she kept her gaze low. She did not have the same confidence as her sister and certainly did not have the same ease of manner and spirit as Rose did! Hyacinth was well aware of her failings, for it was something that her mother had told her fairly regularly. It had not been easy for her to step into society as she had done and hiding herself away so that Rose might take the attention of the various gentlemen that surrounded them had seemed to be the very best of situations.

Though her mother had been greatly displeased – though her father, the Earl of Coatbridge, had been less so.

He had shrugged and said very little, given that he was of a similar nature to Hyacinth herself.

"You hid away! You became a wallflower! And I expect that you have every intention of doing such a thing again, do you not?" Her mother shook her head firmly. "No, no, Hyacinth, you shall *not* be permitted to do that again. It was shameful enough to have my daughter regarded in such a way by the *ton* and my *only* saving grace was that Rose did so well." She lifted her chin. "Indeed, if your father had permitted it, I am sure I would have had her wed last Season! Which might, in fact, make my present situation a little less of a strain."

"I know what you want from me, Mama, but I cannot give it!" Hyacinth protested, feeling a shudder run through her as she imagined herself laughing and smiling the way that Rose did. "I do not have the same confidence!"

"The only thing you lack is beauty." Lady Coatbridge's gaze sharpened. "That is the only thing about you that you cannot change. Everything else can be learned."

Hyacinth closed her eyes, tears lodging in her throat. Her mother did not understand, did not appear to even *want* to understand all that Hyacinth felt and all that she struggled with. It appeared to Hyacinth that the only thing her mother desired was for both of her daughters to marry and to marry well.

Regardless of how it came about.

"I cannot pretend to be someone that I am not," Hyacinth tried to say, though her mother quickly dashed those thoughts away with a wave of her hand. "Mama, I cannot be Rose!"

"Yes, you can!" Her mother strode forward, reaching down to cup Hyacinth's chin and gaze down into her eyes, her expression set. "Hyacinth, I will *not* have you protesting that you cannot do what your sister does. It is a matter of learning, that is all! And you can do all that is required of you, because there is no other choice but to do so. I hope that you can understand that."

Hyacinth swallowed hard, wishing that she could find a way to tell her mother that she was quite wrong, that no amount of learning would change what she could or could not do, but from the fierceness in her mother's eyes, Hyacinth understood that there was nothing expected of her aside from agreement.

"Now." Releasing Hyacinth's chin, her mother stepped away and began to gesticulate again. "There are a good many things that you must not only practice but do consistently, once we are in London. You will have to behave just as your sister does. That means standing tall, smiling brightly, and speaking to *every* gentleman that comes to speak with you. You must exude confidence but not arrogance, show yourself to be genteel but also interesting – *more* interesting than other young ladies! That is the only way you will be able to capture the interest of an upstanding, high-titled, and wealthy gentleman."

Hyacinth closed her eyes, fighting tears. She did not *want* to marry a gentleman who had only a high title and good fortune! That was part of what pushed her back from society, part of what turned her away from it all. The last thing she desired was for her father and mother to insist that she marry a gentleman who had nothing good in him aside from his fortune! She wanted a gentleman of good character, one who was gentle and considerate, one who would understand her shy nature and rather than shun her, welcome it. Most of all, Hyacinth considered, she wanted to marry a gentleman who saw worth whenever he looked at her. It was clear by now that her mother only valued appearance, for Rose was always well-spoken of and delighted in. She, on the other hand, was not considered on the same terms and all because she lacked her sister's beauty. Rose, thankfully, was not of the same mind though Hyacinth had noticed how much her sister reveled in the attention given to her from not only their mother but also the gentlemen who had come to seek her out. She was never unkind to Hyacinth but nor was there any real closeness. The things lacking in her life at the present moment were all what she desired to find within her marriage, should she be blessed with one... but her mother appeared to think of the entire situation in a very different manner.

"You did not answer me, Hyacinth!"

Realizing too late that she had been stuck in her own thoughts and had not been listening to her mother, Hyacinth searched her mind for an excuse. "I apologize, Mama. I – I was only thinking about what you had said." She raised her eyes carefully, relieved to see her mother nodding slowly, clearly believing what Hyacinth had said.

"I am glad to see that you are considering it all, at least." The Countess' eyes flashed with warning and Hyacinth looked away. "Though there is not much to consider, truth be told! Either you will do as I ask or, as I have just said, your father and I will arrange a suitable match for you. Your second cousin, mayhap, for he has been looking for a bride and – "

"Not Geoffrey, Mama!" Hyacinth's eyes flared in horror. "He has already divorced one wife and you know how much of a stain that brings to one's reputation!"

Lady Coatbridge sniffed. "I must think about the shame that would befall me, should I fail to secure marriage for both of my daughters."

"You already have my brother married and I am sure

that you will have no difficulty when it comes to Rose!" Hyacinth exclaimed, suddenly finding herself on her feet though she had not had any intention of speaking to her mother in such a sharp manner. "Why are you so insistent that I must marry? Can you not see how troubled I am by the notion? Why is it that I must pretend to be someone that I am not and marry someone who does not know who I truly am? Why will you not permit me to do as I wish, to settle into society in the way that is secure for me rather than forcing me to do as I cannot?"

The moment Hyacinth finished, she knew she had spoken much too bluntly, much too forcefully. The glint in her mother's eye had grown, a sharpness there which made Hyacinth shudder. There was a tightness about the Countess' lips and though her voice was low and quiet, it made Hyacinth's whole body tremble.

"How dare you speak to me in such a manner?" Lady Coatbridge came a few steps closer to Hyacinth though Hyacinth did her best to remain steadfast, knowing that nothing she had said had been, in itself, disrespectful. Her manner, however, had been much too forward for the Countess.

"You have no understanding of what it is like to be a mother who *must* find all of her children suitable matches," the Countess hissed, her face very pale now save for a deep red spot on either cheek. "It is one's duty and you stand here, complaining at my attempts to improve you?"

Hyacinth did her best to hold her mother's gaze. "I – I do not think that I need improving," she whispered, though the whirlwind that met her words had her whole body shaking furiously.

"Improve?" The Countess laughed bitterly. "Out of all three of my children, you are the *only* one who requires improvement – and the one who ought to be working hard to do as I ask!" Shaking her finger in Hyacinth's face, the Countess glared at her. "I have told you before that you are lacking! And yet, you do nothing to change those weak parts about your character!"

Hyacinth hung her head, having nothing to say in defense of herself. She had tried and, in the face of her mother's fury, had failed entirely.

"You think that you know best when, in truth, you know nothing," the Countess continued, her face slowly turning a furious shade of scarlet. "You do not know anything about society, aside from what I have told you and the *little* you have experienced – and that is your own failing! *I* have your future in mind and yet all you do is complain! I have had quite enough, Hyacinth."

Her eyes closed as a single tear dripped to her cheek.

"Now, you will remain here and consider all that I have said until the dinner gong sounds," the Countess finished, her voice seeming to fill the room. "And you *will* improve your outlook, not only towards society but also to me and all that I am seeking to do for you. Else there will be severe consequences."

With that, she swept out of the room, leaving Hyacinth wondering what it was her mother had meant about consequences as she fought back her tears. Slowly sinking into her chair, Hyacinth covered her face with her hands and dragged in slow gulps of air, having no desire to appear at the dinner table with a tear-stained face. That might mean that her sister and mayhap their father, if he was not too much taken up with business affairs, might notice and ask her about what troubled her so.

Such a conversation would not be a pleasing one.

Squeezing her eyes tightly closed so that she would not

let another tear fall, Hyacinth sucked in a breath and slowly let her hands drop back to her lap.

How am I meant to do all that my mother is asking of me?

It was not a question that Hyacinth had any answer for, nothing came tumbling into her mind that would bring her peace and relief. Instead, there came only fear, doubt, and dread. Fear that she would fail, doubt that she would, in any way, be able to change her character, and dread over all that would befall her if she did not.

This truly was going to be an utterly dreadful Season.

CHAPTER ONE

"Ho there!"

Samuel, the Marquess of Thorne, grinned as not one but three of his friends approached him, clearly eager to see just how well he had done at the card table.

"My friends!" Chuckling, he spread his hands out wide, showing the stack of coins and the one vowel. "What say you to this?"

"Goodness, it appears that you have not only taken *our* money but the money of every gentleman present at the table this evening!" Lord Jedburgh said, pushing one hand through his hair as his eyes rounded just a little as he took in the sheer amount in front of Samuel. "It is clear that you have had an excellent night."

"One of the best," Samuel agreed, with a broad grin. "Though I did feel a little guilty taking coin from my dear friends, however."

This made his friends laugh wryly, each exchanging a glance as though they wanted to be sure that the other felt the very same way. None of them believed for a moment that Samuel had felt even the smallest twinge of guilt over the games he had played and the money he had taken.

"Indeed," Lord Sunderland said, one eyebrow arching. "If you do feel so truly guilty, then I would be glad to alleviate that guilt by retrieving my coins." His eyebrow fell back into place, only to pull into a frown. "I have lost rather a large amount this evening."

"Though that is entirely your own fault," Samuel remarked, getting up from the table and sweeping the coin into a leather pouch, choosing not to give even a small amount back to his friends. "You were the one who sat down to play cards in the first place! Besides," he continued, sending a wink in Lord Sunderland's direction, "it is not as though you cannot afford to lose." Lord Sunderland, Samuel knew, was one of the wealthiest gentlemen in London, though he had a lesser title than Samuel himself.

"That is certainly true," Lord Elledge agreed, chuckling. "Come now, do not be a poor loser, my friend." He set one hand on Lord Sunderland's shoulder. "We all know just how much you do not like to lose any sort of coin but alas, in this case, it appears that you *have d*one so. And there is nothing you can do to regain it."

"Aside from play again." Lord Sunderland shot Samuel a quick look. "What say you? Another game?"

Samuel shook his head. "No, not this evening." Setting the pouch in his pocket, he made his way from the table, his friends following him. "Though another time, certainly."

"I shall hold you to that!" Lord Sunderland stated, slapping one hand on Samuel's shoulder, as though this would be enough to force Samuel to play another game very soon. "You know that I shall not forget."

Though I might refuse all the same. Samuel, disliking

the way that Lord Sunderland was insisting upon this situation, shook off his friend's hand. "Come now, tell me about this soiree. I did not expect there to be so big a crowd, I confess it. Lord Berkshire does not have the largest townhouse in all of England, that much is certain!"

"Though he is still an excellent host," Lord Jedburgh added, with a small shrug when Samuel looked across at him. "I have found this evening to be a particularly enjoyable, even if I *did* lose some coin to an old friend." With a grin, he nudged Samuel, who laughed.

"There will be many more opportunities for you to lose more of your coin to me, Jedburgh. Have no concern in that regard!"

"I thank you." Lord Jedburgh chuckled quietly. "My goodness, this is a good evening, is it not? The card table was open from the very moment we walked into the room!"

Samuel, making his way through the room slowly, began to nod as he took in the sheer number of guests and the footmen who were trepidatiously making their way in and out of the groups of guests with trays of both food and drink in their hands. Given that the card room had been open from the very moment that Samuel had stepped into the room – and since he had made his way there at once – he had not realized just how many other people were present. Their host certainly had invited a good many gentlemen and ladies!

"The library is available, as is the ballroom," Lord Elledge told Samuel, glancing all around him as Lord Jedburgh stepped into another conversation. "It is such a crush in here, I am sure that the ballroom would be less so."

"Indeed." Samuel, who did not much like the crush of a filled drawing-room, began to make his way to the door. "The ballroom, then?"

"The ballroom." Lord Elledge led the way and Samuel followed, with Lord Sunderland falling behind, having delayed to stay and talk with a young lady of quality. Samuel glanced back over his shoulder, wondering who it was that he was talking to but his view was quickly broken up by the faces and figures of others. Lord Sunderland, as far as Samuel knew, had no intention of seeking out a bride this Season, so why was he pausing to talk to a young lady? Recalling the way that Lord Sunderland had behaved last Season, Samuel groaned inwardly. Surely his friend had learned his lesson by now?

"You look thoughtful."

Samuel smiled briefly. "I am merely wondering if our dear friend is considering courting a young lady this Season, despite his protests that he wants nothing like that whatsoever!" He darted a look towards Lord Elledge but his friend only snorted.

"Lord Sunderland will be just as he was last Season, I fear and will be quite determined with it. The only thing that he desires is fine company and if that is with the young ladies present this evening, then I do not think he will have any difficulty in finding it."

This made Samuel frown. "I do not think that I should like him to take advantage of any young lady, especially if they are unwed. After last Season, I would have thought he knew to stay back from them all."

"Nor should I like him to do so," Lord Elledge said, gently. "But we can do nothing at this present moment. And it may very well be that he does nothing at all, aside from conversation and dancing, just as any gentleman of the *ton* might do."

Samuel frowned but did not disagree. Though Lord Elledge was quite correct, there was something about Lord

Sunderland's character that Samuel had always found difficult. There was a streak of determination that ran a little *too* deep, for Samuel had seen Lord Sunderland force others to give him what he wanted on prior occasions. He could only pray that it would not be so today.

"Here we are now." Lord Elledge let out a long breath. "A little less of a crush here, is it not?"

Samuel looked around the ballroom, nodding in quiet agreement. There was entertainment here also – a small quartet that was playing something quite lovely and a dancer or two who were putting on an excellent performance, given the small group that was gathered to watch. Samuel let his gaze rove around the room, noting the one or two smaller groups standing together, though most were of ladies rather than ladies and gentlemen together. He did not want to interrupt them though he was interested in observing them, nonetheless. Being a Marquess with an excellent fortune meant that he was very often in demand when it came to his company and conversation but on evenings like this, Samuel preferred to be very careful and considerate as to which of society he spoke with. That way, he considered, he would be seen as a boon to any conversation, with those involved in conversing with him feeling almost a sense of privilege in what they had been able to do by having him in their company. It was, he knew, a way of adding to his own sense of superiority but that did not much trouble him.

"You are thinking as to who you might go to speak with, I presume?" Lord Elledge, one of Samuel's closest friends, nudged him lightly. "Might it be that you yourself are seeking out a bride this Season?"

Samuel snorted at this, rolling his eyes in as obvious a manner as he could. "I think not."

"No?"

"No." Samuel shook his head firmly. "No, I shall *not* be pursuing a bride."

"And whyever not?"

Lord Elledge, the only gentleman in Samuel's close circle of friends who was already wed, came to stand a little in front of him, forcing Samuel's full attention to be on him. "Why should you turn away from the thought of matrimony?"

With a heavy sigh that, Samuel hoped, told his friend that he had no interest in continuing on this conversation, Samuel spread his hands out. "I have determined that I will marry only when I have no choice but to do so. That may come from a sense of duty from within – though it is not something that concerns me as yet – or it may come from the expectation of others." His hands fell to his sides. "I want only to enjoy the Season, to flirt outrageously whenever I please, and dance, speak, and smile with as many young ladies that will indulge me. The truth is, I can see that matrimony only as a bind, something that would take away all my delight and happiness."

"I hardly think that is true!"

"Well, of course you would say so," Samuel continued, waving away his friend's protests. "You *must* say so, for else it would make out that your present situation is a good deal more miserable than you have tried to make us all believe!" He wiggled his eyebrows and grinned though Lord Elledge's expression soon darkened. "Come now, you *cannot* tell me – and I will not even believe it if you do – that marriage has made you happier!"

Lord Elledge drew himself up, a sharpness in his gaze which forced Samuel's grin to fade just a little. "I should like to inform you, whether you trust me or not, that marrying my dear Eliza has been the most wonderful thing I have ever done. It has brought me more joy and delight than I can express."

Resisting the urge to roll his eyes again, Samuel tipped his head, assessing his friend's expression.

"I will admit that the marriage was not something that I thought well of at the time," Lord Elledge admitted, shrugging lightly as his gaze pulled away. "I am sure that you recall very well the number of times I expressed my frustrations that a gentleman such as I had no other choice but to marry."

Samuel nodded. "Indeed I do."

"But that has changed in this last year," Lord Elledge continued, a firmness in his expression now. "I find myself more than contented, for it has changed my entire world! My whole life is now one of brightness and beauty, and if I am to be truthful – though no doubt, you will mock me for it, I have discovered myself to be quite in love with her."

This knocked all sense of humor from Samuel's chest. Instead, he swallowed hard, blinking quickly as Lord Elledge nodded, perhaps seeing Samuel's shock. The astonishment of hearing such a thing from Lord Elledge shook Samuel's frame entirely, for he had always thought – as had Lord Elledge, he had believed – that love was nothing more than some preposterous nonsense that mayhap, only the foolish young ladies might believe to be real and true. Now, however, it seemed that all of that had been turned entirely on its head!

"I shall not permit you to ask me any questions as though you will find a way to force me to reconsider my feelings and realize that all I have felt is not so," Lord Elledge continued, firmly. "I did not tell you this before for I knew precisely the reaction you would have and I will not permit you to do so now."

"I shall do nothing of the sort." Samuel, who had a thousand questions on his mind in a single moment and wanted nothing more than to throw them at his friend one at a time, swept into a bow. "I assure you, I shall say nothing. It is entirely your own situation and circumstances and if you say that you have fallen in love with your wife, then I have no choice but to believe you."

Lord Elledge lifted his chin. "Good."

"Though I am sorry that she is not here in London," Samuel continued, a tiny hint of a smile touching the edge of his mouth. "I should like to hear from *her* whether or not such feelings are returned." He chuckled as Lord Elledge frowned heavily. "For who could think to fall in love with *you?*"

This made Lord Elledge roar with something mixed between frustration and good humor, though Samuel only grinned. His friend rolled his eyes and then stepped back, looking all around the room.

"I think I could do with another drink." He lifted his chin, gesturing behind Samuel. "There is Lord Sunderland." A small frown pulled at his forehead. "Careful now, I think that he is approaching a young lady standing alone."

Samuel turned quickly, seeing that what Lord Elledge had seen was indeed what was happening. "You go and find us a drink," he said, beginning to step away. "I shall make sure Lord Sunderland does not behave poorly." Quite why a young lady was standing alone, Samuel did not know but he certainly did not want Lord Sunderland to be anywhere near her. Though Lord Sunderland was someone he considered a friend, he did not think well of the gentleman when he was in his cups and thereafter, flirting outrageously with any lady he set his eyes on! And particularly debutants ought, to his mind, be left entirely alone – though Lord Sunderland did not have the same consideration.

"Sunderland! Come with me, if you please." Taking the arm of his friend, he tried to pull him away from the young lady, who was standing against the wall but with huge, frightened eyes that were fixed entirely upon Lord Sunderland. "Come now, my friend. Lord Elledge is finding us the finest brandy."

Lord Sunderland threw out one hand towards the young lady, settling it on her shoulder though she flinched instantly. "You cannot mean to drag me away from this beautiful creature, surely?"

"My – my sister will return in a moment, I am sure." The young lady's voice was quiet but her face was filled with fright. "She is gone only to fetch us both a drink."

"Of course."

"I – I should not like you to think that there was any sort of impropriety." The young lady's breath hitched as she looked into Samuel's eyes and in an instant, he realized what it was that she feared. Instantly, he shook his head.

"No, of course not. I can assure you that no-one will say a word, for there has been no impropriety. Though Lord Sunderland ought to be behaving a good deal better than he is at present!" Relief flickered in her eyes, though her gaze quickly went back to Lord Sunderland. Samuel did not know what it was that Lord Sunderland had said to her in the few minutes before he had arrived but given her expression, he believed that it was not anything good. He was glad, at least, that he had been able to relieve her fears; the fear that someone might think her behaving improperly in entertaining a gentleman's conversation when standing alone.

She was doing nothing wrong, particularly if her sister was only just about to return.

"I have behaved perfectly well!" Lord Sunderland pulled his hand away from the lady and turned towards Samuel, who immediately began to wonder just how much his friend had imbibed in the short time between being in their company in the drawing room and thereafter, the ballroom. "I do not think – "

"Ah, there is my sister." The young lady glanced towards Samuel, bobbed a quick curtsy, and then stepped away. "Do excuse me."

The moment she left, Samuel grabbed Lord Sunderland's arm, yanking him a little closer. "Whatever is it that you think you are doing?"

Lord Sunderland's frown was one of confusion. "I do not know what you mean."

"Last Season, you almost ruined a debutante and it was only because the gentleman courting her wanted to marry her that you were not forced to step in." Samuel gritted his teeth, a flash of upset crashing through him as he remembered all that his friend had done. It had not been a pleasant Season. "Why are you behaving so foolishly now?"

Lord Sunderland rolled his eyes and stepped back, forcing Samuel's hand from him. "You worry too much, Thorne. Keep to your own affairs."

"Brandy?" Lord Elledge broke into the conversation, a glass in either hand. Lord Sunderland, however, took one from him, leaving Samuel with nothing, and with a growing frustration, Samuel turned on his heel.

"I shall fetch another," Lord Elledge said quickly. "My friend, I – "

"I shall be quite all right," Samuel answered, hurrying away from his friends, a dark cloud of frustration twisting around him. This was his first soiree of the Season and yet, somehow, Lord Sunderland had managed to almost ruin it entirely.

I shall not help him again, he told himself, suddenly desperate to be as far away from his friend as he could. *No matter what happens, I shall stay far from whatever trouble Lord Sunderland puts himself in.*

CHAPTER TWO

"Might I ask you something?" Hyacinth glanced towards Rose as they waited in the line to greet the host of this evening's ball. "Yes, if you must."

Her sister looked at her curiously, her brown eyes warm. "What was it you were scribbling earlier this afternoon? You told father that you were writing to Lady Eve but I am not certain that is true."

"It is quite true." Hyacinth lifted her shoulders and then let them drop. "I was writing to Lady Eve. She should be present this evening." Lady Eve was a dear friend of Hyacinth's, with the two families connected for many a year. Her father, the Marquess of Bath, had long been acquainted with Hyacinth's own father and thus, the friendship had continued down the family line.

"You are always writing something to Lady Eve," Rose continued, sounding a little plaintive, her eyes darting away from Hyacinth's. "You have such a close friendship, I confess that I am a little jealous."

Hyacinth said nothing to this, not quite certain what it

is that she *ought* to say. It was true that she and Eve had been dear friends for many a year even though Eve was a little older than Hyacinth, and closer in age to Rose. But that, Hyacinth knew, came from the fact that both she and Eve were similar in character whilst Rose was quite different.

"Why must you always be writing to her?" Rose continued, sounding a little childish now. "It is difficult for me that I have no one to write to, while you are always sending notes here and there."

Hiding a smile, Hyacinth looked away. "I am sure that you will have a good many friends here very soon, Rose," she murmured, a little surprised at the sense of joy that filled her in realizing that her sister did not, in fact, have all the good things in life. "It is not as though you were entirely alone last Season." *Though I was.*

Eve had not been in London last Season, due to the marriage of not only her brother but also her elder sister. With two weddings in one summer, Eve had resided at home and though Hyacinth knew that she had found the weddings to be both beautiful and thoroughly delightful, she had missed being in Hyacinth's company. Not that she had any desire to be a part of the *ton* however, which was precisely the same way that Hyacinth herself felt!

From that, however, had come a little game that, to this day, both she and Eve continued. It had begun as a riddle, sent to her friend to entertain her while all the arrangements for the weddings had taken precedence. It had grown since then, so that both sent each other word puzzles, riddles, and all manner of confounding questions, each trying to best the other.

Thus far, neither of them had been unsuccessful in any puzzle given them, though the last one Eve had sent her had taken Hyacinth a good few days to decipher. That was why she had been 'scribbling', as Rose had put it, for she had been quite determined to come up with the answer before the ball this evening. Having sent it to her friend, she now only had to meet with her to confirm that the answer was correct. Then it would be her turn.

"I do hope that you will not do as you did last evening."

Hyacinth, pulled from her thoughts, looked sharply at her sister. "I beg your pardon? I did nothing wrong last evening. Whatever are you talking about?"

Rose lifted her chin a little, the very same glint that Hyacinth often saw in her mother's eye coming into hers. "You were standing alone, talking to *two* gentlemen! And you told me thereafter that you were not introduced to either!"

Shock rifled through Hyacinth's chest. "Rose, you know very well that I had no choice!"

"You did have a choice, however," Rose continued, astonishing Hyacinth all the more with her sharp tongue. "You could have come with me as I went in search of a drink. Instead, you insisted on staying at the back of the ballroom and let me walk off alone."

"You were not alone," Hyacinth answered, quickly, her heart beginning to hammer painfully. "You were in company with Lady Henderson. You were perfectly chaperoned."

Rose tilted her head. "But *you* were not."

Hyacinth did not know what to make of this, staring back at her sister in utter astonishment. Rose had never been unkind like this before, had never shown any sort of cruel disregard for the difficulties that Hyacinth had when it came to making her way into society. Why was she being so now?

"It is just as well that I did not tell Mama about what happened." With a small sniff, Rose arched an eyebrow. "I know very well that she would be deeply upset with you if she was to know what you had done."

Her mouth going dry, Hyacinth held her sister's gaze, trying to ascertain what it was that Rose was doing by saying such things. Could it be a hint of jealousy? Could it be that what they had been speaking about before as regarded Lady Eve and the many letters that Hyacinth shared with her was the cause of Rose's envy? Hyacinth could think of no other reason and that made her heart fill with pain.

"I do not think it would be wise to put any sort of enmity between us, Rose," she said, slowly as the line began to shorten, bringing them closer to their host. "I do not know why you would say such a thing to me! I thought that you understood what I found difficult and indeed, delighted in all that you garnered from my absence!"

Her sister looked away. "I do not know what you mean."

"You had the attention of almost every gentleman upon you and I did not take any of that from you," Hyacinth answered, speaking quietly so that their mother, who stood in front, did not hear. "Why would you speak to me so now?"

Rose tilted her head, studying Hyacinth with cold eyes. "I have heard mother's concern. She has told me that your absence from society, and your standing as a wallflower could damage my chances of a successful match and that is what I want, Hyacinth. I want not only a successful match but an *excellent* one. When you behave as you do, you bring shame to not only yourself but also to me."

Hyacinth's heart tore but there was nothing she could say in response to this, nothing that she could give to her sister by way of answer. Swallowing at the ache in her throat, she turned to look at the line in front of her rather than trying to speak, seeing now a fresh new callousness in Rose that had been entirely absent before now.

Soon, they were in the ballroom and Hyacinth, in an instant, felt panic grab a hold of her and hold on tightly. The room was filled with all manner of gentlemen and ladies and, seeing them all only made Hyacinth's heart pound with fright. The way that Rose moved with ease into the crowd, smiling and laughing in a single moment was something that Hyacinth simply could not do, feeling as though her feet were pinned to the floor. Her chest tightened, her stomach knotting as she gazed after her mother and sister, wondering if either of them would turn around and notice her absence.

They did not.

"There you are! I have been waiting and waiting for your arrival!"

The nervous anxiety that had torn through Hyacinth in an instant faded just as quickly as it had come. "Eve!" Throwing her arms around her friend in what was, most likely, a less than proper manner, Hyacinth let out a long breath of relief. "Thank goodness you are here."

"Oh?"

Stepping back just a little, Hyacinth closed her eyes and tried to smile, aware of a sudden sense of sadness washing over her. "My mother has demanded that I do not behave as I did last Season, and my sister has, only at this very moment, in fact, told me that I bring her nothing but shame when I stand apart from the *ton*." Opening her eyes, she saw Lady Eve's expression darken. "Neither of them seem to understand my struggle."

"Though they are very quick to tell you of your failings,

I am sure." Lady Eve frowned heavily. "Where are they now?"

Hyacinth swallowed at the knot in her throat. "They stepped away and, no doubt, expected me to follow but I struggled to put even one foot in front of the other. Now that you are here, however, I will find things a little easier, I am sure."

Lady Eve smiled. "Then I am very glad that I insisted that I wait by the door for you."

Smiling back, Hyacinth took in another long breath to steady herself, her gaze darting around the room. "And where are your own parents?"

Lady Eve shrugged. "My mother is somewhere with my new brother-in-law and my sister is just over there, showing everyone her wedding ring." She rolled her eyes and laughed. "Though I must say, I can understand why she does so, her husband loves her dearly and gifts her the most beautiful diamond and the like!"

"I see." Hyacinth slipped her arm through her friend's. "I have been told that I must marry this Season. I must find a suitable match, though quite how I am to do so when I find myself so upset even by stepping into a ballroom, I do not know!"

"I will help you." Lady Eve smiled, though, to Hyacinth's eyes, it faltered a little. "There is something more I must tell you, my friend."

"Oh?" Pausing in their walking around the ballroom, all thought of mothers and sisters and chaperones forgotten, Hyacinth looked back at her friend carefully, wondering what it was that troubled her. "Is there something wrong?"

Lady Eve closed her eyes for just a moment. "I am engaged."

It felt as though Hyacinth had dropped through the floor and crashed into the darkness beneath.

"I did not make the choice myself but it was my father's arrangement," Lady Eve continued, as Hyacinth tried to drag air into her tight lungs. "I was informed of it only last week and I did not want to write to you about it. Instead, I thought I would tell you when I was in your company."

"Engaged?" Hyacinth breathed, as Lady Eve nodded. "But why? I thought that you – "

"Would be able to make my own choice?" A tinge of pink came onto her cheeks. "In a way, I have."

Thoroughly confused, Hyacinth frowned. "What do you mean?"

A small breath escaped from Lady Eve, though she also began to smile. "As you know, last Season, I was not in London. I spent it at my father's estate, given the preparations for the wedding." She glanced away. "During the course of that time, I was introduced to Lord Wiltshire."

"Wiltshire?" Hyacinth repeated, the name sounding a little familiar. "I remember him – is he not the brother of Lady Livinia, the lady your brother chose to wed?"

Lady Eve nodded. "Yes, that is so."

Hyacinth's eyebrows lifted. "You are engaged to Lord Wiltshire? And your brother is wed to Lord Wiltshire's sister?"

Pressing her lips together for only a moment, Lady Eve nodded again, though there came a slight sparkle in her eyes, one that spoke of happiness – and Hyacinth felt herself slowly lifted out of the darkness that had captured her.

"You are happy, then?" she asked, relieved when Lady Eve smiled brightly. "You have been able to make your own choice?"

"I believe that my father saw that there was a connection between us and *he* was the one who initiated all manner of discussion between himself and Lord Wiltshire," Lady Eve told her, beginning to walk again as the first dance of the evening was announced. "When he told me that Lord Wiltshire had agreed to marry me, I must confess that I was not only surprised but a little upset that there would be no courtship or the like. However, my father, in his goodness, permitted me to have some time before my marriage so that I might get to know Lord Wiltshire a little better – an engaged courtship, if you will."

"And that is why you are in London?"

Lady Eve spread out her other hand. "He is here somewhere! We are to dance later this evening and I must confess that I am already looking forward to it."

"I am glad for you," Hyacinth answered, truthfully. "I am truly delighted to know that you will be happy."

With a small, gentle smile gracing her lips, Lady Eve looked back at her. "I think I shall be, yes... though that also means that I am able now to help you as much as I can! We shall conquer the *ton* and find you an excellent match."

Hyacinth shook her head. "I do not think it will be as easy as that, my dear friend," she murmured, aware of just how much fear still lingered in her. "My mother has made it plain that I not only lack my sister's beauty, I also lack her poise and her ability to capture the attention of the *ton*. I do not know what it is I can do if I am already so much of a failure!"

"You are *not* a failure!" Coming to a dead stop, Lady Eve turned to face Hyacinth directly. "I will not pretend that you are the very same as your sister, for that would be disingenuous, but you are certainly not plain! Nor do you lack poise! Besides which, you have a good many things that your sister does not and that ought to be something you take confidence from."

Hyacinth looked away, not certain that what her friend said held any truth.

"Think about the riddles and the puzzles you have sent me and I have sent to you," Lady Eve continued, taking Hyacinth's hand and pressing it, hard. "I have found them so very difficult that I have, on occasion, been forced to ask others to help me!"

This was news to Hyacinth and her gaze swung back around to her friend, who nodded to confirm it.

"You, no doubt, have not asked anyone," Lady Eve said, as Hyacinth smiled just a little. "You have an incredible mind, my dear friend and that is something that your sister does *not* possess. She is much too taken up with fripperies and flirtations, which, in themselves, are not a bad thing but are different from the joys that *you* seek out. That is not to say that yours are in any way worse than your sister's or that she is in some way better than you, only that you are both *different* from the other and that should not be used to set you apart." She scowled. "Even though I am well aware that it does."

Hyacinth, feeling her spirits a little lifted, smiled warmly. "Thank you, Eve. You do know what to say to make me feel a little better and I am grateful for that." Her smile grew as something Lady Eve had said settled into her mind. "Were you speaking the truth when you said that you had asked others about my riddles?"

Lady Eve chuckled. "Yes, I did speak the truth. I was so very frustrated with your last one that I had to go to my father to have his help and even then, I was struggling!"

"Riddles?"

Another voice broke into their conversation and

Hyacinth's spirits quickly dropped as Rose appeared beside her, their mother only a few steps away.

"I am sure that I would be able to solve any number of riddles," Rose continued, turning her head to look up at two gentlemen who had come to join them. "What do you say to that, Lord Thorne? Lord Elledge?"

"Riddles?" Lord Elledge shrugged. "I am not so good at such things, I confess. I have no time for them!"

Lord Thorne, a gentleman that Hyacinth recognized, chuckled. "Oh, I am *very* capable when it comes to such things. I do not think that I would have any difficulty whatsoever!"

Any feelings of warmth that might have filled Hyacinth upon seeing the gentleman again – the gentleman that had taken Lord Sunderland from her at the soiree – evaporated in an instant when she heard his arrogance. Exchanging a look with Lady Eve, she forced a smile but said nothing, choosing to keep her love of riddles and word problems entirely to herself.

"I should introduce you, should I not?" Rose smiled but there was a slight sneer in it, as though she was proud of the fact that *she* was the one who was introducing Hyacinth to not only one but *two* gentlemen whilst suggesting silently that Hyacinth would never have been able to do such a thing.

"I am already acquainted with one of these fine gentlemen," Hyacinth found herself saying, seeing Rose's smile slipping as she gestured to the gentleman she knew. It would have been wise not to have said such a thing, she knew, for she did not know the gentleman's title but nor could she bear to see Rose's arrogance being pushed towards her yet again.

"And how is that?" Rose exclaimed, turning to both

gentlemen. "How is it that you can be acquainted with Lord Thorne when I am not?"

"Your sister and I were acquainted at a soiree," Lord Thorne said, easily, though there was a hint of surprise in his expression which Hyacinth could not help but feel a little embarrassed about. "We did not have the pleasure then, however."

Rose's face turned a shade of pink which spoke of both anger and embarrassment, though she kept a smile placed upon her lips which, to Hyacinth's mind, must have taken a great deal of strength.

"I see. Then I shall introduce you to Lord Elledge, Hyacinth." Rose gestured to the other gentleman, who quickly bowed. "Might I present the Earl of Elledge? Lord Elledge, this is my younger sister, Hyacinth."

"How very good to meet you."

Hyacinth smiled and dropped into a curtsy, thinking that Lord Elledge appeared to be a very amiable gentleman given the warmth of his smile and the softness about his expression. "I am glad to make your acquaintance."

"And I am already acquainted with you, Lord Elledge," Lady Eve remarked, as Hyacinth rose from her curtsy. "And also with you, Lord Thorne." She bobbed a quick curtsy but, to Hyacinth's surprise, did not smile. "How good to see you both again."

"It has been a pleasant Season thus far, has it not?" Lord Elledge remarked, the warm smile still on his face. "My dear wife insisted that I come to London to enjoy some respite from the business of my estate matters and I must say, I think she was quite correct to do so!"

Rose blinked quickly, twisting her head around to look hard at Lord Elledge. "Your wife is here in London?" The surprise in her voice told Hyacinth that she had believed

Lord Elledge unattached. "I – I am surprised we were not introduced."

"That is because she is *not* in London, in fact." Lord Elledge smiled though, to Hyacinth's eyes, there was a hint of sadness there. "She has gone to spend a few months with her sister, Lady Crawfield. *Her* husband, Lord Crawfield, has gone to the continent on business affairs and my dear wife did not want to think of her sister all alone. Thus, she has gone to Scotland and, though I was invited, she urged me to come to London and enjoy some time here." He chuckled, his eyes twinkling. "I think that secretly, she intends to make sure that I miss her so very much, I will be all the more devoted to her – even more than I am at present!"

Hyacinth smiled gently, seeing that Lord Elledge clearly cared for his wife a great deal. It was a lovely thing to see and not something that she had often heard expressed.

"I see." Rose, evidently regaining her composure, turned her attention instead to Lord Thorne, the only unattached gentleman present. "You must be very glad to have your companion present in London. It is clear you have a very strong friendship."

Hyacinth resisted the desire to roll her eyes, wondering quite how her sister was able to comprehend such a thing after such a brief connection.

"It does bring me contentment, yes." Lord Thorne tilted his head, regarding Lord Elledge. "Though I am quite certain I would have been able to have an enjoyable Season without his presence, all the same."

Surprise filled Hyacinth's chest, only for Lord Elledge to laugh, making her realize that this was said solely in jest.

"Ah, but who else would be able to bring you to the company of such fine ladies and encourage you, thereafter, to dance?" Lord Elledge said, sending a wink towards Lord Thorne. "I do hope you are all dancing this evening?"

Hyacinth flushed hot, her dance card quickly held behind her back. She had not stepped out to dance with any gentleman in the previous Season and had no desire to do so now – but how could she escape this now?

"Of *course* we are!" Rose exclaimed, though as she slipped her dance card from her wrist, she shifted her stance so that only she was facing Lord Thorne, leaving Hyacinth hidden from him. Dropping her head in embarrassment over her sister's clear actions, Hyacinth shot a quick look towards Lady Eve, though she was frowning.

"Lady Eve, Lady Hyacinth?" Lord Elledge, though he also looked to Rose as he spoke, though no expression other than his smile lingered. "I should very much like to dance, I think, if you would oblige me!"

Hyacinth knew that she had no other choice but to accept him, for it would be utterly improper for any young lady to refuse a gentleman. Swallowing hard, she swung her hand out from behind her back and handed it to him, wishing that she did not have to.

"I thank you."

"Oh, Lord Thorne, might I ask you if you would be willing to fetch me a glass of ratafia before we dance?"

Hyacinth's heart twisted as she heard her sister vying for Lord Thorne's attention, pulling him away from Hyacinth herself before she even had a chance for her dance card to be taken.

"But of course, I should not mind in the least," she heard Lord Thorne say, before walking away from the small group – though Rose quickly sent a small smile towards Hyacinth as she turned around to join her.

"It is not as though you would be asked for a dance

anyway," she murmured, as she came to stand beside Hyacinth. "You know that you do not have my beauty nor my poise."

Those were the very same words that Hyacinth had heard from her mother time and again but this time, they cut her to the quick. They had never been close as sisters but neither had Rose ever been cruel.

It seemed as though things were going to change between them, Hyacinth realized, though she certainly did not like the change.

In fact, she feared it was going to be more painful than anything she had ever experienced before.

CHAPTER THREE

Samuel yawned as he stretched out across the *chaise longue,* a tray with coffee and a selection of delicacies beside him. He had enjoyed a sennight of entertainment and last evening's soiree had been one of the finest of the Season thus far. Though this morning, he had awoken with an aching head and a creeping sense of fatigue which had forced him to take the morning very slowly and quietly indeed.

"'The London Chronicle,'" he murmured, holding up the paper and beginning to read. It was not often that he read the papers but this morning, he felt the need to do so. It was a quiet pursuit and after all that he had been enjoying these last few days, it was exactly what he needed. First, he read some news regarding one of the most important bookshops in London, reading that it was going to change hands. Next, he took in a drawing of Lord and Lady Sommerville, finding himself smiling as he took in the sketch. It was certainly recognizable, though some of their features were a little exaggerated. Thereafter, there was an article on the history of Wrexham, which he enjoyed reading very much.

And then, he came to a riddle.

With a frown, Samuel read it once, twice, and then pushed himself up on his elbow. Why could he not find the answer to this?

Mumbling the words aloud, he frowned and rubbed at the spot between his eyebrows, trying to understand.

"I intrude upon moments but with unseeing eyes. I witness your strife but I cannot speak my advice. Frozen in time, I linger on, never to death but perhaps forgotten. What am I?"

Sitting up straight and ignoring the sharp stab of pain in his head from doing so, Samuel's frown grew as he read the lines for the fourth time. It was a clear riddle, one where he was meant to come up with an answer – or mayhap, see the answer clearly – but he simply could not.

"It must just be because I am tired," he told himself, reaching to sip his coffee. With a grimace, he looked back again at the riddle. There was no name to it, no one stating that this was their creation. Quite why the author had chosen to remain hidden, Samuel did not know but that was not the source of his frustration. It was more the fact that he simply could not seem to find the answer.

Setting the paper down, he reached to pick up one of the cakes on the tray, hoping that some food might encourage his thoughts to center on the riddle and provide him with the answer.

Nothing came to him and, becoming all the more irritated, Samuel let out a low growl and flung the paper away. It was nonsense and nothing more. He did not need to let it trouble him, did not need to let it bite away at his mind as though it was some sort of irritating fly that he could not get rid of. He was tired, that was all. His head ached and he had not eaten a great deal this morning.

Those were the cause of his inability to find the answer to the riddle.

"And it means nothing," Samuel told himself aloud, reaching for his coffee again. "I am sure that very few others in the *beau monde* will have taken note of this." *And those that have will, no doubt, find themselves in the very same position as I. I am quite sure of it.*

∼

"Well?"

Samuel frowned as Lord Sunderland barreled towards him, practically knocking into Samuel. "Good evening, Lord Sunderland."

"Good evening." Lord Sunderland grinned broadly, his eyes moving from face to face, making Samuel feel a trifle uncomfortable. "Might I ask whether you are enjoying this evening?"

Shrugging, Samuel took a sip of his brandy. "Lord Ingilston has, to my mind, taken a little too long to open up the card room but aside from that, I am enjoying, yes."

"And no doubt you have heard of the riddle, yes?"

At this, Samuel stiffened, though he kept his gaze forward. "I beg your pardon?"

"The riddle!" Lord Sunderland exclaimed, speaking so loudly that one or two others turned their heads to look at them. "Surely you have heard of the riddle? It was in 'The London Chronicle' this afternoon and everyone is speaking of it! It has quite captured the attention of many of us, I assure you!"

"Oh." Samuel sniffed and attempted to express disinterest. "I did see it but I did not spend much time thinking on it."

"You did not?" Another voice spoke to his left and Samuel turned sharply, about to express to whoever it was that he had not had any inclination to set his mind to the riddle, only to see a fair-haired young lady smiling back at him, her blue eyes vivid in color. Her companion smiled up at him also, though she had dark hair and green eyes.

Samuel's stomach turned over on itself. "Good evening to you both," he said, wondering if he had already been introduced to them and had forgotten their titles. "Might I ask if – "

"A quick introduction, mayhap?" Lord Sunderland chuckled, coming around from Samuel's other side to reach out one hand towards the two ladies. "Miss Marshall and Lady Susanna, might I present the Marquess of Thorne?" A glint came into his eye as he set his gaze to Samuel, his interest in the ladies clear. "Lord Thorne, this is Miss Marshall, daughter to Viscount Dunnett and Lady Susanna, daughter to the Earl of Kingslaw."

Samuel bowed low. "How very good to meet you both. " He was truly quite delighted to be introduced to such beautiful young ladies though the question one had asked still riled him. "As I was just saying to my friend, I did see the riddle but I did not set my mind to it."

Lady Susanna glanced towards her friend, then smiled. "I am sure that you would have found the answer the very moment you set your mind to it." She sighed and shook her head. "Alas, I do not have the answer as yet."

"Nor I," Miss Marshall added, fanning herself just a little as her face grew a little pinker. "Though I should very much like to know what it is."

Lord Sunderland chuckled and leaned in closer. "I might be able to help you there."

"Oh?" Lady Susanna sounded surprised, sweeping a

quick look towards Samuel. "That is most interesting, Lord Sunderland. Though, before you tell us the answer, I do wonder if you, Lord Thorne, might have any insight? Any clue that you might wish to give us that would help our considerations?" She giggled and nudged her friend lightly. "I know that Miss Marshall wants the answer but I think I would be contented to think on it a little more, especially if I was to garner some understanding from either of you gentlemen?"

Samuel forced a smile, wishing that he was more than able to sweep in with the correct answer to the riddle for then, he might find himself in favor with both of these two young ladies. He was always seeking out new acquaintances, though he had no intentions of courtship or the like, of course. It was only because he enjoyed being in the company of fine ladies and all the more appreciated their interest in *him*. The way they came to speak with him, eyes darting this way and that, smiling at him from under lowered lashes as teasing glances were sent back and forth... all of that made him feel as though he stood head and shoulders above the other gentlemen in London.

Except now, it seemed, he was to be shamed by none other than Lord Sunderland, a gentleman who had nothing akin to the excellent reputation that Samuel possessed!

"No?" Lord Sunderland sounded quite astonished, his head turned in Samuel's direction. "I would have thought that you would have something to share, Thorne!"

Samuel drew himself up as tall as he dared, refusing to let himself be shamed. "I am certain that I would have some insight to give, had I paid any attention to this riddle! The truth is, I do not even remember what it is about!"

"Oh, then I shall tell you, if I might?" Miss Marshall beamed at him as though she were doing him some great favor, leaving Samuel more than a little frustrated. "I memorized it, you see?"

"Of course." Samuel's smile did not linger as he wanted it too, feeling his lips pull downwards, revealing his frustration though thankfully, Miss Marshall did not seem to notice. "I should be very glad to hear it."

"Then here it is." Closing her eyes, Miss Marshall recited the riddle word for word, just as Samuel remembered it. "I intrude upon moments but with unseeing eyes. I witness your strife but I cannot speak my advice. Frozen in time, I linger on, never to death but perhaps forgotten. What am I?"

What was he to do but to consider it? Rubbing one hand over his chin, Samuel let the words run through his mind, trying to think of an answer – any answer – which he might give to the young ladies.

Silence was his only response. His mind would not give him what it was he wanted, not even now when these young ladies were waiting for him!

"*I* think it is an object." Lord Sunderland spoke before Samuel had time. "A very particular object."

The two young ladies gasped and Samuel scowled, seeing how they both took a step closer to Lord Sunderland.

"Do you know what it is?" Miss Marshall was now looking up at Lord Sunderland with slightly widened eyes, clearly amazed by him and his supposed wisdom, which made Samuel's embarrassment begin to grow.

"I do." Lord Sunderland said it with such confidence that even Samuel wanted to ask him what it was exactly, though he forced himself to remain silent. "I confess that I did have to think on it for some time before I was able to understand what it was, but once I did, it was very easy indeed."

Lady Susanna's breath caught in a gasp, her eyes rounding at the edges. "You found the answer that quickly, Lord Sunderland?"

Samuel, aware that he was behaving rather poorly, turned on his heel and made his way across the room, as if he had seen someone that he very much wished to speak to and, as yet, had not been able to do so. That was not his aim, however. His only desire was to make his way as far from Lord Sunderland and the two ladies as he could. Shame haunted his every step, mortified that he could not appear to find the answer to the riddle while Lord Sunderland could. Why was it that he simply could not find the answer if Lord Sunderland had discovered it in such a short space of time? He had never considered Lord Sunderland to be a particularly learned or wise fellow and yet, here he was, proving to Samuel and the others in the *ton* that he was more than capable of such things!

At least he is not speaking anything inappropriate to these two ladies, he thought to himself, reaching for a fresh brandy and then making his way out of the room and to the terrace, intending to stand outside for a few minutes. *That is a relief at least.*

"You look a little frustrated, Lord Thorne."

The moment fresh air brushed across Samuel's cheek, so did yet another remark. He was about to tell the young lady that he did not need her observations before making his way from the terrace and stepping back inside, only to notice the slight curl at the edge of her lip.

"Lady... Hyacinth, is it not?" A small frown tugged at his brow. "Your sister is Lady Rose."

"Yes." She did not smile and no sense of warmth effused through her words. "That is so. You danced with her some nights ago."

"But not with you."

Finally, she smiled but no light came into her brown eyes, the darkness of her hair seeming to send sweeping shadows across her expression. "You did not ask me, Lord Thorne."

That made fire light in his chest, sweeping up into his face as he scowled.

"My sister is just standing over there, if you wish to speak with her." Lady Hyacinth, either not seeing or choosing to ignore the look on Samuel's face, gestured behind her. "My mother also."

Samuel took a mouthful of his brandy but said nothing, his eyes on Lady Rose. She had been an enjoyable conversation, with good conversation and skill in dancing, but he had been left with a sense of dislike in his chest once she had stepped away. On consideration, it had been, to his mind, because of her over-eager remarks, the too-bright smile, and the near constant fluttering of her eyelashes. Yes, he wanted young ladies to enjoy his company and to seek him out but there were those who were a little *too* keen and she had been one of them.

"If you must know, I have become irritated with the inane chatter about this blasted riddle," he told her, though the surprise which leaped into her eyes must, he assumed, have come from his sudden change of conversation. "You have heard of it, no doubt."

"The riddle?" Lady Hyacinth blinked, a small frown across her forehead. "I have not, no."

"Then you are the only one who has not," Samuel stated, seeing her frown grow though he ignored the fact that he had been a little rude in such a statement. "Have you not heard of 'The London Chronicle'?"

She nodded.

"Then the riddle is contained within."

Lady Hyacinth swallowed, a paleness in her cheeks now which Samuel presumed came from the slight chill in the evening air. "Might I ask what it was?"

Instantly, the riddle came back into his mind with full clarity, making Samuel's irritation burst into him anew. Try as he might, he could not seem to escape it! "It says something akin to, 'I intrude upon moments but with unseeing eyes. I witness your strife but I cannot speak my advice. Frozen in time, I linger on, never to death but perhaps forgotten. What am I?'"

Lady Hyacinth caught her breath and a cold hand gripped Samuel's heart. "Surely you do not mean to say, Lady Hyacinth, that you know the answer to this riddle so quickly?"

Again, she blinked but she did not look at him. Instead, her gaze was very far away, going to the wall over his shoulder rather than coming anywhere near his face. The coldness that gripped him ran all the way over his skin, fearful now that he truly was the dunce.

"Lady Hyacinth," he said again, a little more loudly this time which, in one moment, made Lady Hyacinth not only start in surprise but turn her gaze to his again. "Might I ask if you know the answer?"

The moment she began to nod, Samuel's gut began to twist painfully. He narrowed his eyes a fraction, trying to tell himself that she was only saying so to make herself appear knowledgeable, but the clearness in her expression made him doubt that.

"You know the answer," he said again, as the edge of her mouth began to lift. "Are you quite sure?"

"Oh, I am *more* than certain." Lady Hyacinth's voice was firm, making it quite plain that she was quite determined in her response. "In fact, I should not doubt for even a moment that I am wrong."

"Then you must tell me." Lifting his chin, he held her gaze with a bravado he did not really feel. "That way, I can tell you for certain whether or not you are correct."

A flickering frown darted into her expression, her eyes holding his but with a slight narrowing of the edges. Samuel said nothing, holding his stance and praying silently that she would give him what he required. Yes, it was a falsehood on his part to state that he knew the answer already and would be able to confirm with her whether she was correct in her thinking, but he certainly was not about to admit that he did not know it! That would bring him more embarrassment than he was willing to shoulder. What he felt within himself at this present moment was already more than enough.

"Very well." Lady Hyacinth's smile edged up all the more. "Though why do you not tell me what you think first, Lord Thorne? I should be glad to know what answer *you* give to the riddle, for then I will be able to keep my mortification to myself, if I am wrong." Her smile grew and Samuel had the distinct impression she knew very well what he was trying to do. "After all, are not gentlemen meant to be more learned in all things compared to a young lady such as myself?"

Samuel's mouth went dry as he struggled to find a response to give her; one that would bring about what *he* desired while, at the same time, making sure that he did not give himself away. "I suppose that your considerations in that is quite correct," he agreed, seeing her smile fade just a little. "Therefore, it would not do for me to give you the answer first. It would make me appear arrogant and egotistical, I think."

"Oh, I do not think so."

"But I do," Samuel spoke quickly, interrupting her before she could make any further excuses. "Please, do tell me what you think. It may be that you *have* the answer after all and have nothing to concern yourself with!"

A small sigh whispered from her mouth as she held his gaze steadily, perhaps feeling that she had no more excuses to give. With a lift of her shoulders, Lady Hyacinth spread out her hands. "Is not the answer quite obvious?"

"I suppose that it is, yes." Sniffing, he held his head high. "I was able to decipher it within a matter of moments."

"Indeed."

He nodded but said nothing, still waiting. Lady Hyacinth smiled again, the expression irritating Samuel though he forced his expression to remain outwardly calm.

"It is a portrait, is it not?"

Relief poured onto Samuel as though he had just stepped out into torrential rain. It ran in rivulets over him, a wide smile spreading immediately across his face. "A portrait! Of course!" The smile shattered as he saw her lift an eyebrow. "You are quite correct, Lady Hyacinth," he added hastily, fearing now that he had given himself away entirely. "That is the very answer I had. It seems that you have done well in this."

"So it would seem," she murmured, tipping her head just a little as she studied him, making Samuel feel distinctly uncomfortable. Shifting from foot to foot, he quickly inclined his head, deciding to step away so that he might share his knowledge – or tease some young ladies with his knowledge of the riddle.

"I should leave you to your mother and sister now, I think," he said, as Lady Hyacinth's eyes narrowed, giving Samuel the impression that she could read his thoughts and see his intentions, even without him saying a single word to her. "Do excuse me, Lady Hyacinth. It has been a pleasure talking with you." This last sentence was not true in the least, of course, but Samuel did not care. Well aware that he was being a little rude, he scowled and walked away, his sense of mortification heightening with every step. He knew full well that he had not managed to hide his lack of answer from her, that she had seen through his falseness and realized precisely what it was he was doing. What made him all the more upset was that *she* had managed to get the answer in a matter of moments whilst he had been struggling continually!

Irritated and finding no enjoyment from the soiree any longer, Samuel thought about leaving, only to turn and make his way to the card table instead. Perhaps he could find a little happiness there, finally able to forget all about that blasted riddle.

CHAPTER FOUR

Hyacinth sent a sidelong look towards her friend as Lady Eve finished her ice. Thus far, Lady Eve had said nothing about the riddle and The London Chronicle but Hyacinth was quite certain that *she* was the reason behind it all.

"I do love Gunters," Lady Eve sighed, smacking her lips and then smiling at Hyacinth. "Thank you for joining me."

"Thank you for the invitation." Hyacinth sighed and sat back in her chair. "My mother has been berating me near incessantly these last few days, telling me that I am not doing as she has asked."

"Though you have tried not to be a wallflower," Lady Eve protested, defending Hyacinth even though her mother was not present. "*And* you are often in my company."

Hyacinth sighed. "That is true but it is not enough. She wants me to be dancing every dance, just as Rose does. She wants gentlemen to be calling upon *me* though none have as yet."

Lady Eve smiled sympathetically. "I am sorry for the struggle you are having. That must be difficult."

"It can be. Though," Hyacinth continued, speaking carefully now, "there has been *some* respite to our conversation at times, for my mother has been speaking about the riddle that has everyone in the *ton* so excited." She arched one eyebrow as a blush rose in Lady Eve's cheeks. "I recognized the riddle when Lord Thorne told me of it, for it was one that I myself had written."

"Is that so?" Lady Eve smiled but her gaze darted away from Hyacinth. "How very interesting."

Hyacinth laughed despite her attempts to have her friend tell her the truth. "Eve, I know very well that *you* must have been the one who sent in that riddle, for I wrote it to you."

"Very well!" Sounding exasperated, Lady Eve threw up both hands, though her lips curved at the very same time. "I know I ought not to have done so without your consent but I wanted to encourage you." Her smile softened. "After what you said about your sister and your mother and the way that they speak both to you and of you, I could not help it. I wanted you to see that you *do* have some marvelous qualities and that yes, though you may be different from Rose, that does not make you any lesser."

A growing appreciation settled in Hyacinth's heart. "I am not in the least bit upset, I assure you," she said, quietly. "Though I did not know that that was your motivation. Truth be told, that has truly touched my heart."

"I am your friend!" Lady Eve exclaimed, reaching forward to touch Hyacinth's hand for a moment. "And I will do all that I can to defend you, of course." The color in her cheeks heightened. "Even if it does mean sending in your riddle to The London Chronicle in the hope that it will be published!"

Hyacinth chuckled, shaking her head. "I did not think

that my riddles would ever be in the minds of the *beau monde*! I am even more astonished that someone such as Lord Thorne did not have the answer."

"Lord Thorne?" Lady Eve frowned. "He is an arrogant gentleman and if I am to speak truthfully, I would state that I have very little kindness in my heart towards him. Indeed, I think him almost the very worst sort of gentleman and would advise you to stay far from him. He is not a fellow who is in any way inclined towards matrimony but still pursues the young ladies of London so that he might get their attention fixed upon *him*." She sighed and shook her head. "I do not like gentlemen who only think of their own importance."

"Thankfully, your betrothed is not that sort of fellow." Hyacinth, having already been introduced to Lord Wiltshire previously, had thought him a very kind, amiable sort who, given his long looks towards Lady Eve, did indeed seem to be quite taken with her. "He seems to give a great deal of thought to your every need!"

Lady Eve smiled and tilted her head just a little. "No, he is not egotistical in the least," she said, a touch wistfully. "He is quite the opposite in fact." Perhaps seeing Hyacinth's small smile, Lady Eve gave herself a small shake. "Though we were speaking of Lord Thorne, were we not? What is it that he said to you?"

Quickly, Hyacinth recounted the conversation, telling her friend just how she had been able to discern that Lord Thorne had not known the answer to the riddle but that he had pretended that he had done. "It was quite foolish of him, for had he simply admitted that he did not know the answer then I would have had a good deal more respect for that."

"He tried to have you give him the answer so that he

would know it and then be able to tell others." Lady Eve rolled her eyes. "No doubt he would not have been pleased that you had it before he did!"

Recalling the frustration that had leaped into Lord Thorne's eyes when she had made it clear to him that she knew what the correct answer was, Hyacinth chuckled softly. "Indeed, though he did attempt to hide that from me as well – though he could not. His every emotion is written into his expression, though I do not think that he realizes that."

"Most gentlemen do not." Lady Eve giggled, clearly fully aware that she was making a sweeping gesture. "It is clear to me that Lord Throne was displeased that you discovered the answer before him, though mayhap that ought to take the strength of his pride down just a little."

With a small smile, Hyacinth shrugged. "I do not know whether it will or not."

"But if he does not get the answer to the next one, then – "

"The next one?" Hyacinth repeated, as Lady Eve quickly nodded, her eyes alight with all manner of thoughts. "What do you mean?"

Lady Eve blinked in surprise, perhaps having not expected Hyacinth's response. "You cannot think only to write one riddle, Hyacinth!"

"I only wrote those riddles for *you*," Hyacinth answered, her stomach turning over on itself as she realized what Lady Eve meant. "You cannot think that I would write more simply for The London Chronicle?"

"But why not?" Lady Eve protested. "It is the first time in a *long* while that something like this has captured the *beau monde* in such a way. While they are normally thinking only of gossip and rumors, they are now discussing this riddle, trying to ascertain which of their friends worked out the answer before them and, so I have heard, eagerly hoping for another so they might pit friends against each other once more!"

This was not at all what Hyacinth had suggested. Having heard her mother and sister speaking of the riddle as well as Lord Thorne, she had realized that it had interested some, but she had never expected it to be to this extent!

"I will not tell anyone that it is you who writes them," Lady Eve continued, clearly trying to reassure Hyacinth. "I will send them to The London Chronicle on your behalf, if you wish. Why, I think if you were to send two or even three riddles at one time, they would all be printed!"

"Three?" Hyacinth gasped, a small shock panicking her heart. "Eve, I do not know if I can come up with even one!"

Her friend chuckled, giving Hyacinth a smile. "My dear friend, I have *all* the riddles that you have ever written to me! I keep them in a particular box and have brought that box to London. I am sure that, if you wish, we can look through them together and decide which ones to send in. What say you to that?"

There was no reason for her not to agree, Hyacinth could see that, but all the same, reluctance held her back. What if someone discovered that it was her who had been writing these riddles? What if her mother found out? She was already failing in her mother's eyes and the dread that she might be flung in the direction of her disgraced second cousin was already a burden.

"Your mother and father will not discover it." Lady Eve, evidently able to read Hyacinth's mind again, leaned forward and pressed her hand to Hyacinth's arm. "I promise you that."

Hyacinth licked her lips and then slowly nodded. "So long as it is kept quite secret." Her eyes closed tightly as an unexpected tear pressed against her lashes. "I have not told you as yet but my mother has threatened to marry me to Geoffrey." When she opened her eyes, Lady Eve's face had gone very pale indeed.

"The baron?"

Nodding, Hyacinth's throat began to ache. "Baron Goodrich. The one who divorced his wife simply because he became bored with her."

Her friend blinked rapidly, only to then toss her head. "I do not believe it."

"Believe what?"

Lady Eve lifted her chin a notch. "That your mother would *ever* marry you to that lout! Do you not see that the disgrace it would bring the family were you to be connected to him?"

Hyacinth shook her head. "You do not understand my mother, I think. She has told me that the disgrace of having an unmarried daughter would be worse than the disgrace such a connection would bring."

"And you believe that?" Lady Eve sounded astonished and Hyacinth quickly frowned. "I do not think that your father would ever permit that." Her head tilted just a little. "Tell me, did she say such a thing in front of your father?"

Trying to recall, Hyacinth slowly began to shake her head no.

"Then I would consider that nothing more than an empty threat, Hyacinth." Curling her hand into a fist, Lady Eve thumped it lightly on the table. "Put it from your mind and do not let it concern you. And, if it should come to it, I swear to you that I shall protest at the wedding itself, stating that I have heard rumors that the baron's divorce has not truly been completed and thus, you shall be free of him."

Hyacinth could not help but laugh at this and, as they both rose from the table, she took Lady Eve's hands in her own. "Thank you for your encouragement, my friend."

"But of course."

With a smile, Hyacinth turned to make her way from Gunters. "Another riddle then, yes?"

"Two, I think!" came the exclamation behind her. "If not three, as I have said."

Considering for a moment, Hyacinth smiled. "Two, then. And I shall look forward to seeing if Lord Thorne can decipher *these* especially."

CHAPTER FIVE

There she is.

Try as he might, Samuel could not seem to forget Lady Hyacinth. No matter where he went, he was either thinking of her and the supercilious smile she had sent him when she had realized his lack of success with that riddle, or he was setting his eyes firmly upon her without having had any real intention of doing so. What made matters worse was that two new riddles had appeared in The London Chronicle only the day before and Samuel had not yet managed to decipher either of them! He had told himself that he did not care, that he ought not to give his time and attention to such foolishness but all the same, it gnawed away at his mind, just as Lady Hyacinth did.

It was all most frustrating.

"Whatever is wrong?"

Samuel glanced towards Lord Jedburgh. "Good afternoon, Lord Jedburgh."

"You are frowning." Gesturing to Hyde Park, the many people present and the beautiful sunshine, Lord Jedburgh turned his gaze back towards Samuel. "What is it that has made you so displeased? Could it be the sunshine? The fine summer's day? Or is it the number of ladies present that has upset you? Mayhap you were expecting more?"

Samuel snorted, trying to hide his irritation and Lord Jedburgh's gentle mocking. "I am not in the least bit upset."

"Your expression says otherwise."

Rolling his eyes, Samuel threw a glance towards Lord Jedburgh's grinning face, only to shrug. "It is of no consequence. I was lost in thought for a moment, that is all."

Lord Jedburgh chuckled. "Dare I ask what it was you were thinking of? Or is that to be quite private?"

It was not as though Samuel could say that he had been thinking of Lady Hyacinth and becoming frustrated with himself for his own inability to pull his thoughts away from her. Instead, he only shrugged and looked away from Lord Jedburgh, choosing not to give any answer whatsoever.

"You will not tell me?" Lord Jedburgh sounded disappointed which, surprisingly, confirmed to Samuel that he had been right not to say a word. Lord Jedburgh was one inclined towards gossip and the like and Samuel was not about to give him any fodder for such things.

"*I* know what he was thinking."

With a scowl launching itself onto his face, Samuel turned to Lord Elledge who had stepped out of the gathered crowd to join him. "Good afternoon, Lord Elledge. I believe that you are intruding on a conversation between myself and Lord Jedburgh."

"Yes, indeed I am." Lord Elledge chuckled, showing no regard for Samuel's clear frustration. "As I was saying, Lord Jedburgh, I know the reason that Lord Thorne is so upset."

"Is that so?" Lord Jedburgh, his eyes flickering with

interest, turned towards Lord Elledge, coming to a complete stop rather than ambling through the park as they had done before – and Samuel too was forced to come to a stop. "Then pray inform me, for Lord Thorne will not and I confess, I am concerned for him."

Samuel snorted at this. "I hardly think that is true."

Lord Jedburgh feigned an injured look but said nothing, still gazing at Lord Elledge in clear expectation.

"It is because of these 'blasted riddles' as I have heard him say on more than one occasion," Lord Elledge told them both, making Samuel's eyebrows lift high. "He is frustrated by them, confounded and upset. Though he does attempt to hide them."

Samuel drew himself up at once. "That is absolutely *not* the case."

"Yes, it is."

"The riddles?" Lord Jedburgh asked before Samuel could attempt to defend himself further. "You speak of the ones that have been in The London Chronicle, yes?"

Jutting his jaw forward, Samuel sliced the air with both hands, trying to bring an immediate end to the conversation. "Lord Elledge is mistaken. That is not at all what upset me." That, at least, was quite true, for it was not the riddles that had been sitting in his thoughts as he had walked through the park. It had been Lady Hyacinth – but to admit to that was not something Samuel was prepared to do, not even if it would convince Lord Jedburgh and Lord Elledge that he was *not* caught up entirely with these riddles.

"You know the answer to them both, then? Or is the opposite true?" Lord Elledge's eyebrow lifted. "My assumption is that, given your present frustrations, you have not had any success?"

Lifting his shoulders, Samuel let them drop. "I do not give much thought to these riddles," he said, in what he hoped was a less than interested tone. "I am aware that everyone in the *ton* is speaking of them but I have very little desire to linger on them, study them, and answer them."

Lord Jedburgh began to laugh, his eyes dancing. "Oh-ho! Then it is true, what Lord Elledge says, is it? You are not able to answer them!"

"Good afternoon, gentlemen."

Before Samuel could say another word, the arrival of not one but three young ladies prevented him from saying so.

"You must forgive us for interrupting your conversation," the first young lady said – a Miss Fortescue, if Samuel remembered correctly – as she bobbed a quick curtsy. "But we did overhear you speaking of the riddles and thought that we simply *must* come to find out what your answers are to them both!"

Lord Elledge grinned broadly, turning his attention squarely upon Samuel, so that all three ladies – one of which, Samuel noted, was none other than Lady Hyacinth – all looked to him also. His stomach dropped, a light sheen of sweat breaking out across his forehead as he shuffled his feet and tried to think of what to say.

Then, an idea came to him. It was not without risk, certainly, and could put him in a great deal of difficulty but it was the only way that he could escape these questions... and escape the knowing look on Lady Hyacinth's face.

"Well, Lord Thorne?" The third young lady, Lady Eve, if Samuel remembered correctly, put both hands to her hips in a less than proper manner, her eyes flashing with something that was either humor or mockery. Samuel could not tell. "What have you to say?"

It was on the tip of his tongue to start speaking the lies that were in his mind but a warning held him back. Taking in a deep breath, he spread out both hands. "I have not seen these two new riddles, I confess. That is to say, I have read them, of course, but – "

"Oh, but Lady Eve has committed them both to memory!"

Much to Samuel's surprise, Lady Hyacinth spoke up in such a clear and determined manner, that it stole away his breath for a moment. Yes, they had been in conversation before and yes, she had not held back from the conversation then but there was something new in her voice now. It was as though she wanted to catch him out, wanted to see him acknowledge his defeat and failure.

Samuel's heart lurched, nausea climbing up his throat. *No. I cannot permit that.*

"Oh, yes, I have!" Lady Eve exclaimed, throwing a smile towards her friend which, Samuel saw, Lady Hyacinth returned with a wink. "Let me tell you them now."

That wink made Samuel's whole body flush with heat. He knew, right then and there, that Lady Hyacinth and Lady Eve had the answers to both riddles already... and that yet again, he did not.

"Here is the first: I have no mouth and yet I can speak. I have no ears but still, I can hear. I have no body nor soul, but for a moment, in the wind and the air, I come alive." Lady Eve smiled around the group, and Lord Jedburgh quickly nodded.

"Yes, I have that one. Remind me of the second?"

"But of course." Lady Eve glanced towards Samuel, then tore her gaze away again, the edges of her mouth quirking. "The second is as follows: there is a family who live in an estate just outside of London. A girl in that family has as many brothers as sisters, but every brother has only half as many brothers as sisters."

Lord Jedburgh screwed up his eyes tightly. "I do not think I can even understand that one!"

Miss Fortescue laughed and set a hand to his arm for a moment. "Wait, Lord Jedburgh! It is not finished yet."

Lady Eve spread out her hands wide. "The question is, how many brothers and sisters are there in the family?"

Samuel blinked, fighting the urge to drop his head into his hands. That riddle was one that completely and utterly befuddled him, and yet even though Lord Jedburgh was able to admit it, he simply could not. It would break apart his pride, would shatter the very heart of him if he were to state that no, he had no answer for either riddle. The one thing he adored about society was being admired and there certainly would come no admiration should he admit to that!

"It took me some time, but I did work out the answer to that one," Lord Elledge said, as Lord Jedburgh let out a low groan. "I did see that The London Chronicle printed the answer to the previous riddle in this edition. I must hope they will do the same for these two so that I can be quite sure I am correct!"

Miss Fortescue giggled. "I spent an hour with my tea and cake making sure that I had the right answer for that last one! Mayhap, Lord Elledge, you might tell us of *your* answer so that I can know if I am incorrect or not! I confess I am too ashamed to tell you my thoughts for fear that I will be ashamed."

"Is that so?" Lord Elledge shot a look towards Samuel, one that was filled with meaning but Samuel ignored it as best he could, feeling heat begin to crawl up his neck. "You say you have no interest in these riddles, Thorne? Though you have read them?"

Wishing that his friend would not attempt to tease him so mercilessly in front of young ladies, Samuel scowled at him but Lord Elledge only grinned. With frustration still building, Samuel dropped his head, squeezed his eyes closed and took in a breath.

And then, he spoke.

"There is a specific reason that I take such little interest in the riddles," he said, speaking in a low, soft tone that made all three ladies move a little closer. "You all believe that I do not know the answers but it is, in fact, precisely the opposite."

Lord Jedburgh frowned. "You mean to say that you do know the answer to these two riddles but have chosen not to tell us of that?"

Samuel nodded. "Precisely."

"And why is that?" Lord Elledge sounded amused, as if he could tell that Samuel was clutching at excuses. "Why would you give the impression that you do not know the answers? Why are you so vague? Why state that you have no interest in them if you do, in fact, have the answer to both?"

The lie forced itself to the front of Samuel's mind and he spoke it without hesitation, praying that what he asked, they would do.

"I shall tell you but you must all swear yourself to secrecy," he murmured, making every other person lean towards him, interest on every face. "You must not tell another person within the *ton* for I do desire this to be a secret."

"A secret?" Miss Fortescue's eyes widened. "Goodness, Lord Thorne, what is it?"

Samuel smiled, though it felt as though something was crawling in his stomach, an inner warning telling him he ought to pull back from this – but it was much too late.

"Because, Miss Fortescue, I have done my best to protect myself. I do not want anyone in society to know that *I* am the one who writes the riddles."

CHAPTER SIX

Hyacinth took a step backward, reeling from Lord Thorne's sudden revelation. Miss Fortescue was instantly at his side, asking questions at two to the dozen, her hand on his arm, her eyes shining.

Hyacinth, however, felt nothing but confusion and, after a few moments, a growing anger.

"You must not tell anyone," she heard Lord Thorne say, as Miss Fortescue nodded fervently. "You have seen that the author does not write their name at the bottom of the riddles, yes?"

Miss Fortescue kept her eyes pinned to his as Hyacinth struggled to know where to look.

"That is because I do not want anyone to know. I have acted foolishly, mayhap, in pretending a lack of interest that I have not truly felt," Lord Thorne continued, letting out a small sigh as though he regretted that. "The truth is, I have been eagerly awaiting the *ton*'s reaction to the riddles and certainly did not ever think that so many would be so eager to answer them!"

Feeling as though she wanted to burst out in anger and

rail at the Marquess, Hyacinth turned on her heel and stalked away, aware that she was acting most improperly but heedless to what might be said of her actions. Her mind was filled with a loud and incessant buzzing that would not cease, seeming to grow louder with every step. She was forced to pull long breaths into her burning lungs, her hands curling into tight fists as she put one foot in front of the other, having very little idea as to where she was going.

"Lady Hyacinth?"

Looking up, Hyacinth took in the concern which spread across Lord Wiltshire's expression. Try as she might, she could not speak, could not put words to all that she felt. With a small shake of her head, she made to step past him but Lord Wiltshire only frowned and moved with her.

"Something is wrong. Besides which, you ought not to be alone at the present moment. Hyde Park is large and – " His gaze went over Hyacinth's shoulder. "Ah, my dear Lady Eve. Good afternoon." Seeming to forget entirely about Hyacinth, Lord Wiltshire stepped away from her and grasped Lady Eve's hand. "How good it is to see you."

"And to see you also," came the reply, though Lady Eve quickly came to stand by Hyacinth who, given her present state of mind, had not taken a single step. "Might you give me a few moments with Hyacinth?"

Lord Wiltshire nodded and returned to his conversation, leaving Lady Eve to stand with Hyacinth.

The concern in her eyes made the anger in Hyacinth's chest fade a little, though it was swiftly replaced with hot tears.

"I certainly did not expect that," Lady Eve murmured, her eyes searching through Hyacinth's expression. "You are upset, of course."

Closing her eyes, Hyacinth took in a shaky breath,

trying to keep the threatening tears at bay. "That was most unexpected. I thought... I thought that when we spoke of the riddles, he might admit to us all that he had not the answers."

"And instead, he has taken the riddles from you entirely," Lady Eve answered, quietly. "It was clear to me that he did not know them again, though whether he gave any time to their consideration, I could not say."

Hyacinth shook her head, her throat working furiously. Keeping her gaze away from Lady Eve's concerned face for fear that it would send the tears she had been keeping back down her cheeks, she tried to speak but her voice rasped terribly.

"It will not stay a secret for long. Others will know soon enough and then the *ton* will believe that it is *his* clever thinking that has provided them with such entertainment."

Lady Eve squeezed her hand. "You could counter it. You could simply tell the *beau monde* that it is your work."

Considering this for a second, Hyacinth shook her head. "No. It is pointless to do so. He is a Marquess and I am a wallflower. If I were to say such a thing when the *ton* has already heard that he has been writing them, then it would only make me appear foolish. No one would believe me."

Lady Eve's eyebrows drew together. "Some would."

A sense of hopelessness began to weigh Hyacinth down, her shoulders dropping. "I am convinced that even my own mother and sister would not believe me, not even if I showed them the riddles I had been sending you for so long." A single tear dropped to her cheek. "I would only shame myself by doing anything."

A visible tremor ran through Lady Eve. "Did I not tell you that he was arrogant?"

"You did." Hyacinth dabbed at her cheek quickly,

sniffing once as she fought to regain her composure. "Though I believed you, I certainly did not ever think that he would do something like this!"

"Nor did I."

Closing her eyes against another wave of tears, Hyacinth squeezed one hand into a fist, trying to calm herself inwardly. She felt as though he had thrown her out into the darkness by taking credit for what she had done, albeit without being aware that *she* was, in fact, the one responsible for writing the riddles in the first place. After all of her elation and excitement at seeing the next two riddles printed in The London Chronicle, she now had nothing but despair and brokenness.

"You must do something."

Opening her eyes, Hyacinth looked dully back at her friend, lacking even the smallest amount of determination within herself. "There is nothing that can be done. I cannot go to him and tell him the truth, for either he will not believe me or, if he does, he will not care."

"That is not what I mean." Lady Eve put one hand on Hyacinth's shoulder. "There must be a way to prove to the *ton* that he is not telling the truth. Even though he has sworn us to secrecy, I have no doubt that Miss Fortescue will tell everyone and Lord Jedburgh also."

Hyacinth's lips lifted briefly. "Yes, I do not think that Lord Thorne's secret, such as it is, will be hidden from the *ton* for long."

"So you must use the riddles to force the truth out of him."

Wrinkling her nose, Hyacinth frowned. "I do not know what you mean."

"Find a way to have him fumbling for answers!" Lady Eve's eyes gleamed. "Or find a way to make them so personal, he is aware that you are upset that he has taken away your glory from all of this! There must be something that can be done so that he does not have all of the *beau monde* pursuing him with delight! They ought to be looking to you, praising *you* for your wisdom and clever thinking, not him."

A thin beam of light pierced Hyacinth's mind, though she struggled to see any real clarity. "I am not certain what could be done."

"You do not need to have the answers now," her friend said, as Hyacinth slowly began to nod. "I am asking you only not to give up. Though... " The smile on her face faded as a frown tugged at her forehead instead. "Though you might have to become a little better acquainted with Lord Thorne. That might mean pushing yourself forward into society a little more."

Fear lurched into Hyacinth's heart. "Why?"

"Because," Lady Eve explained, "if you are to catch him out, then you will need to be able to have conversations with him, and with those in his acquaintance. I know that you do not like stepping into society, I know that you find it difficult but this, mayhap might give you a purpose *aside* from finding a suitable match." Her eyes searched Hyacinth's. "Do you think you could do such a thing? I would do all that I could to help you."

Hyacinth worried the edge of her lip, unsure as to whether she would have the strength to do such a thing. "It would please my mother, I suppose. She might be willing, then, to step back a little from me rather than urge me on or criticize me for my failures at any given moment."

Lady Eve nodded but said nothing.

"I – I suppose I could try," Hyacinth admitted, seeing

the smile immediately light up Lady Eve's expression. "I will need your help, however."

"And you shall have it." Grasping Hyacinth's hands, Lady Eve beamed at her and Hyacinth could not help but smile back, sensing the darkness around her fading now that she had a clear purpose. There was a chance, now, for her to regain her riddles for herself, a chance for Lord Thorne's arrogance to crumble around him as the *ton* realized the truth.

And that, certainly, was worth pursuing with all of her might.

"Lord Sunderland, good evening." Hyacinth's stomach was rolling this way and that as the gentleman who had, at the very start of the Season, behaved so poorly towards her, cast a sharp look over her.

Then, a leering smile spread right across his face. "Ah, Lady Hyacinth." After a moment – and much to Hyacinth's relief – he glanced around the rest of the small, gathered group. "Good evening to you, Lady Rose, Lady Hannah, Lady Millford, Lord Kensington, Lady Gertrude."

Where is Eve?

Hyacinth pressed her hands together in front of her, trying to ignore the creeping sense of panic which was slowly climbing up over her frame. Standing with her sister at this ball had been one thing, for Rose had made it quite clear that she did not want Hyacinth's company – though Hyacinth had refused to acknowledge that and had stood with her anyway. Lord Sunderland's presence, however, was quite another. The way he had spoken to her at the very first soiree she had attended had been nothing but shocking and, truth be told, quite frightening. She had been dreadfully afraid that someone would overhear him and would think that she was, in some way, connected to this rogue but much to her relief, that had not occurred.

The conversation flowed around her and Hyacinth steadfastly ignored the glances that Lord Sunderland seemed to throw in her direction. The last time she had been forced into his company, Lord Thorne had, surprisingly, been the one to rescue her from him. Though she thought him arrogant, selfish, and, a gentleman willing to lie, that had shown her a side of his character that countered the negatives just a little.

Though I highly doubt he would do so again. That sent the corner of her mouth flicking upwards ruefully, fully aware that Lord Thorne did not think highly of her. It had been three days since Hyde Park and his declaration to them all, and it had only been yesterday that Hyacinth had finally sent Lady Eve another riddle for The London Chronicle. Soon, it would be printed and then, she might begin her plan of confronting Lord Thorne about his lies, albeit in a most covert manner.

"You did not speak to me very well the last time we were in conversation."

A hand touched her elbow and Hyacinth started in surprise, pulling herself away from Lord Sunderland, hating the smile which sent a dark gleam into his eye. "That is because you spoke most improperly," she answered, though her voice was kept low for fear that someone would overhear.

"Then permit me to rectify that and your poor impression of me." Lord Sunderland put one hand to his heart and inclined his head, though Hyacinth did not believe for even a moment that he was truly apologetic. "Do you have your dance card, Lady Hyacinth?"

The fear which had surfaced in Hyacinth's heart at his arrival now grew into a crescendo as she blinked furiously, torn between fright and the worry over impropriety. It was not right for a young lady to refuse a gentleman but nor did she wish to be swept up in Lord Sunderland's arms. "I – I do not think – "

"You *are* dancing this evening, are you not?" The gleam in his eye grew as he leaned a little closer to her, making her recoil inwardly though outwardly, she stood stock still. "I do not know why you would refuse me, Lady Hyacinth. That would be most... upsetting."

"That is a nonsense. You are not upset by anything in the least."

A cheerful voice broke between Hyacinth and Lord Sunderland, making the latter frown hard but flooded Hyacinth with relief.

"Good evening, Lord Sunderland, Lady Hyacinth." The gentleman – not someone that Hyacinth thought particularly well of at present – bowed low towards her and then looked to Lord Sunderland, a broad smile on his face. "Are you trying to influence this young lady by pretending you will be upset if she does not stand up with you?"

"Not in the least, Lord Thorne." Lord Sunderland scowled though Hyacinth's breathing grew a little steadier now that he had come to interrupt the conversation. "You know as well as I that every young lady ought to be delighted with every dance that they are offered!"

Lord Thorne's eyebrows lifted high, though he did not look towards Hyacinth. "Goodness, you are very full of yourself at the moment, are you not?"

Lord Sunderland snorted, his lip curling. "That says something, coming from a gentleman such as yourself!"

Hyacinth dropped her head, keeping her gaze on the

floor as she felt the sting of Lord Sunderland's words, even though they were not meant for her. It was yet further confirmation that Lord Thorne was an arrogant fellow, though it seemed that Lord Sunderland was very much of the same ilk. Her eyes darted up for a moment, seeing Lord Thorne leaning close towards Lord Sunderland, saying something in his ear that, given the dark expression that lurched across Lord Sunderland's face, he did not like much.

Lord Sunderland's jaw shot forward. "I think I shall take my leave, then." He glanced at Hyacinth but did not nod nor bow. "Do excuse me."

Her gaze lifted as, much to her surprise, Lord Sunderland moved away almost at once, leaving Hyacinth to stand with Lord Thorne, whilst the rest of the group continued in their conversation.

"Please." Lord Thorne held up one hand as Hyacinth opened her mouth to speak. "There is no need to thank me."

Hyacinth's eyebrows lifted. She had been thinking to say something to the Marquess but it had not been to thank him, for that might have been considered improper. She did not know why he had come over, why he had chased Lord Sunderland away as he had done but she had not thought to express her relief in any way whatsoever!

"I was not about to." A small, stiff smile spread across her face. "I was about to ask why Lord Sunderland stepped away."

"Oh." The proud expression on his face quickly melted away.

"As I had not yet given him my dance card, as he requested," Hyacinth answered, a flush of shame beginning to creep up her neck as she spoke for she knew full well she had not had any intention of dancing with the fellow.

Lord Thorne frowned. "Did you truly wish to dance with Lord Sunderland after all that he said to you the last time he came upon you so... improperly?"

The guilt in her heart would not permit her to lie and, after a moment, she shook her head. "No, I suppose not. But it would not have been right for me, as a young lady of quality, to refuse him. And my mother would not have appreciated my refusal either." Her smile dimmed as she looked away, disliking the smile which quickly ran across *his* face. "Though I do hope that you said nothing on my behalf that pushed him away from this conversation."

Lord Thorne shrugged. "I said what was necessary, that is all. He frowned, his smile gone. "The truth is, Lady Hyacinth, and I do not say this lightly, that Lord Sunderland – as you might well already appreciate – is not a gentleman who always behaves well towards others in the *ton*. Particularly towards young ladies."

"I can understand that." A little surprised that Lord Thorne appeared to be trying to protect her from his somewhat nefarious friend, Hyacinth managed a small, genuine smile. "If I am to be honest, then I will admit to being grateful that I do not have to stand up with him to dance."

Lord Thorne chuckled and, much to her frustration, Hyacinth's heart leaped up high for only a moment. The gentleman was handsome, his dark hair dancing carelessly across his forehead, his blue eyes filled with light. Quickly turning her attention away from him, she tried to reenter the conversation with the others in the group, only for Lord Thorne to take a small step closer.

"I do hope that you would permit me to have your dance card, Lady Hyacinth?"

A twist in her chest at his words made her breath freeze in her lungs.

"Well?"

"Oh, are you to dance with my sister, Lord Thorne?"

Rose's clear voice, holding an edge of surprise, broke through Hyacinth's surprise and fright, making her skin prickle all over as every eye in the group turned towards her.

"I was, yes." Lord Thorne smiled back at Rose, as Hyacinth forced herself to pull her dance card from her wrist. "I have not yet signed a single dance card and thought it was high time I did so."

Rose laughed brightly, as Hyacinth managed to hand her dance card to Lord Thorne, hating how she trembled visibly when his fingers touched hers for a brief second. Dancing was something she knew she *could* do though dancing with a dance master and dancing with an actual London gentleman were two very different things!

"My goodness, Lord Thorne, you'd be best to be gentle with my dear sister." Rose smiled widely as Lord Thorne glanced towards her though Hyacinth closed her eyes, fearing what was to come.

"Gentle?"

"Because she has not danced this Season as yet! Nor even last Season!" Rose exclaimed, as every single person in the group turned their full attention towards Hyacinth, making her flush hot as she caught their astonishment. "She was much too busy trying to be a wallflower, you see."

Hyacinth hung her head, mortified. Her sister was laughing as she spoke, clearly trying to make light of what she was saying but Hyacinth did not find a single word to have any mirth in it whatsoever.

"I am glad, then, to be able to change that." Lord Thorne's voice was gentle and quiet and Hyacinth, unwillingly, lifted her gaze to his. What she saw there astonished her, for there was no trace of any pride, arrogance, or even mockery there in his face. Instead, there appeared to be understanding, the small smile reaching out in comfort. She managed to return his smile with a tiny one of her own, aware of the heat behind her eyes. Lord Thorne offered her a small nod, then wrote his name in one of the spaces on her dance card before returning it to her.

Rose moved towards Hyacinth quickly, pushing into her so that she might look at Hyacinth's dance card. What she saw there astonished just as much as it did Hyacinth, though she let out such a loud exclamation that Hyacinth started in surprise.

"The waltz?" Rose's eyes rounded. "You are to dance the waltz with my sister?"

The Marquess chuckled. "Well, you were the one who told me that I had to be gentle, did you not? And the waltz is the easiest of all dances, I think." His smile grew though he turned his attention to the other young ladies rather than keeping it on Rose. "Is there anyone else that should like to dance with me? I should be glad to step out with any of you all!"

This was met with a flurry of dance cards and Rose, letting out a small squeak of either exasperation or excitement, pushed herself in front of Hyacinth so she too might have Lord Thorne sign *her* dance card.

In the melee, Hyacinth was able to step back, pulling herself out of the group so she might move back into the shadows. Her heart was beating furiously, her whole body alive with both excitement and confusion.

The waltz? Why ever had Lord Thorne chosen her waltz, knowing full well it was the most intimate of all the dances?

He is arrogant, she told herself, trying to make sense of

not only all that had happened but all that she felt also. *He thinks this will make me think well of him, I am sure.*

Try as she might, however, Hyacinth could not be fully convinced by her own arguments. Her lips curved, a small happiness beginning to bubble up in her chest. In front of the gathered group, Rose had tried to shame her, had tried to make her appear foolish and a good deal lesser than Rose herself. But Lord Thorne had come and stepped into the fray, bringing Hyacinth to the fore again and almost raising her over the others.

And for that, Hyacinth could not help but be grateful.

CHAPTER SEVEN

A small frown gathered across Samuel's forehead as he watched the *ton* walk through the London streets. He was busy enjoying an ice from Gunters as he sat in his carriage and, at the very same time, taking in the sights and sounds of London. It was a rare few minutes that he had alone to think for he had every intention of stepping out and joining the other members of the *beau monde* once his ice was finished.

There is Lady Rose.

His brow furrowed as he took in the young lady, watching her walk, arm in arm, with another young lady though the lady he knew to be her mother walked only a few steps behind. Lady Rose had not made an excellent impression upon him, he had to admit. The way she had spoken about her sister, Lady Hyacinth, had made not only Lady Hyacinth deeply embarrassed, but it had also clearly upset her. Samuel had seen the color rising in her cheeks, had noted how she had lowered her head, and let her gaze fall to the ground as the others in the group looked at her in astonishment. Quite why Lady Rose had spoken so, Samuel could not be certain but he believed that her main reason for doing so was to make herself appear a good deal *more* than her sister, so that he – and mayhap others in the group – would be willing to ask *her* to dance, rather than looking towards Lady Hyacinth at the first.

It had not had that impression upon him. Yes, he had taken her dance card and yes, he had danced with Lady Rose but he had not appreciated the fawning delight that appeared to be a part of who she was. Their dance had been filled with conversation and laughter, though it had come, on the whole, from Lady Rose alone. Samuel had to admit that Lady Rose had a good deal more beauty than her sister, with her sparkling green eyes, lily white skin and fair curls that danced every time she took a step, but her character was, to his mind, certainly lacking. Though, he considered, he did not know Lady Hyacinth very well either, and what he *did* know of her, he also disliked.

Or is it that my pride stung and thus, I decided that I did not much like her company?

That made him wince. His failure in character was not something that Samuel readily considered, having already assured himself that his penchant for arrogance was something that all gentleman had to bear and was a trifling concern.

"My lord!"

A call to him made Samuel frown, seeing Lady Rose and her companion now beckoning to him. He had not intended to go to join them and had thought, instead, to wait for slightly better company before he made his way out of the carriage. Now, however, he could not escape them and, with a small sigh, he opened the door and stepped out, leaving the glass from his ice for his ticker to return.

"Lord Thorne!" Lady Rose curtsied quickly, her eyes

filled with something that Samuel could not quite make out. "I have only just heard the news! You must have thought me very rude indeed not to have mentioned it before and in that regard, I am truly sorry."

"The news?" Confused as to what she meant, Samuel could only glance to the other young lady, Miss Fortescue. "What do you mean, Lady Rose?"

Lady Rose gestured to Miss Fortescue. "My *dear* friend has only just informed me that you are the one who has written the riddles!"

"She... " Samuel shot a quick look towards Miss Fortescue, who quickly flushed red. "Miss Fortescue, that was told to you in the strictest confidence!" He knew well enough that what he had said to Miss Fortescue, Lady Eve and Lady Hyacinth would, at some point, escape through the *ton* but he had not thought it would be as soon as this!

"I know that it was, yes," Miss Fortescue answered, looking to Lady Rose as if she required her full support, "but nor could I remain silent! The new riddles in The London Chronicle were exceptional and both Lady Rose and I were thinking just how marvelous they were – and, well, the truth of the matter just slipped from my mouth before I even had a chance to think! I am truly sorry, Lord Thorne. It was an accident, I assure you."

"Though I have not been sworn to secrecy and I shall certainly *not* remain silent!" Lady Rose exclaimed, her effervescent manner all the more pronounced. "Good gracious, Lord Thorne, how could you keep such a thing to yourself? I must know why it is that you did not put your name to your work, for surely a gentleman such as yourself would desire the *ton* to know that you are the one who has put such great dedication into these riddles. That way, they can show you such appreciation as is deserving of your efforts."

Samuel tried to smile, finding himself a little uncertain as to how to answer. He had always known that lying about this would bring him some difficulties but he had not thought as to what difficulties those would be. Now, he realized, he would have to speak lie upon lie if he were to keep the story convincing, and that was a little troubling. He would have to remember what he said to Lady Rose and, if questioned again by another, recall it exactly so he would say the very same thing again.

"I – I confess that I wanted to enjoy the moment," he said, hoping that this would be a reasonable explanation. "I wanted to see just how much the *ton* appreciated the riddles before I told everyone that I had written them."

Lady Rose lifted an eyebrow. "You mean to say that you were afraid that those of us in the *ton* would not think well of your riddles?"

He lifted his shoulders. "It was not something that The London Chronicle had ever printed before and, as I have said, I did not know whether the *beau monde* would like them." Letting his shoulders fall, he quirked his lips, trying to ignore the steadfastly growing worry in his stomach over all the many lies he was telling. "I must say that I was also a little concerned about my standing in society. I did not want to be laughed at, had they not been a success."

Miss Fortescue laughed softly, her eyes glinting. "Now that is something I both accept *and* understand, Lord Thorne. No one in London wishes for the *ton* to mock or tease them, so to take care in this is, I think, quite wise."

Samuel smiled briefly, seeing Lady Coatbridge coming to join her daughter, though she stayed a few steps back. Lady Hyacinth and Lady Eve had joined her, though neither of them came to step forward into the conversation, making Samuel wonder whether they did so as not to interrupt his present conversation or if they simply did not wish to join him.

Though why should I mind if Lady Hyacinth does not want to join us? He thought to himself, as Lady Rose began to speak at length about the new riddles printed in The London Chronicle. *It should not.* He lifted his chin. *It does not.*

"I must say, I did find these new riddles to be rather different from the other ones, but then again, I suppose you did so to make things more difficult for us."

Samuel blinked, pulling his attention back towards Lady Rose. "I beg your pardon?"

"The riddles," she said again, just as Lady Hyacinth and Lady Eve exchanged a glance, surprising Samuel as they both stepped forward as one, coming to join the conversation with seeming eagerness. "They were very different from your other ones. A little more pointed, mayhap? I did wonder if you were using them to point the finger at someone though..." Lady Rose tilted her head coquettishly, a teasing smile on her face. "I suppose, even if that were so, you would not tell me of it."

"Indeed, I would not." Forcing a smile, Samuel gestured to the bookshop behind Lady Hyacinth and Lady Eve, finding himself in a state of nervousness, such as he had never experienced before. Something about Lady Hyacinth's presence, about her nearness to him and the many lies that were pouring out of his mouth was unsettling him to such an extent, that he was now looking for a way to escape. "You must excuse me, I am afraid. I have only a short while until I must return home and I intend to step into the bookshop."

"Oh, but then we shall join you!" Lady Rose exclaimed, only for her mother to step closer.

"Alas, you cannot," she said, smiling her greeting to Samuel. "I must take Lady Fortescue back to her townhouse and you and I are then to take tea, with your father already present at the house. Do you not recall?"

Lady Rose pouted, though Samuel caught how both Lady Hyacinth and Lady Eve exchanged a glance with each other.

"I quite forgot, Mama." Lady Rose frowned, only to then alter her expression entirely when Samuel turned his attention to her again. "I do hope that we can continue our conversation again later, Lord Thorne. I have so much I wish to ask you about your riddles!"

Placing one finger at the collar of his shirt as he nodded, Samuel's feet burned in his boots, urging him to begin walking towards the bookshop and escape them all. "Yes, of course. Do excuse me."

With a nod, he hurried away, relieved to leave them all behind. Stepping inside, he immediately began to meander through the many rows of books, taking in long, steadying breaths.

It did not instantly help his sense of confusion and upset, as he had expected. Regret was beginning to pull in his heart now but he silenced it quickly, reminding himself that he could do nothing to alter what he had already done.

I did not think that I would have to speak so many lies, he thought to himself, frowning. *And what did Lady Rose mean when she said the new ones in The London Chronicle were a little more pointed?*

That made his brow furrow, confused now as to why Lady Rose would have made such a remark. Making his way to the shopkeeper, he quickly asked for a copy of the

London Chronicle and the man hastily obliged him. With a nod, Samuel made his way from the fellow and found, in the upstairs of the shop, a quiet place where he might sit and study the riddles.

He found them quickly enough. One read of them was not enough for him to gain any success in understanding them, cursing himself inwardly for his slow mind. Rubbing one hand over his forehead, he leaned forward in his chair and read the first aloud.

"I am something that ought never to be told, yet I am spoken by both old and young alike. Without a body, I cause great harm, without a knife, I cut many ties. What am I?"

Shaking his head to himself, Samuel muttered darkly over his lack of success, going on to read the second. "I show my face but wear a mask, I walk the path but lead others astray, my words a stumbling guide. The masquerade, my favorite occasion for there, I can be my true self."

That one hit Samuel right between the eyes, his stomach shifting this way and that as he took in the words. A masquerade was a place of hiding, where one could wear a mask and pretend to be someone they were not. They could disguise themselves, hiding away behind a mask and a costume, if it so pleased them.

So this riddle, this word trickery, spoke of someone who wore a disguise, though not only at a masquerade ball. It was someone who 'led others astray' and who did so with their words.

A deceiver.

Samuel closed his eyes, the knot in his stomach growing ever stronger. Could it be that this was as Lady Rose had said? That this was more pointed than before, but it was pointed towards him?

Frowning, he set his mind on the other riddle. Bending

his head, he studied it carefully, heedless to just how many minutes were going past. He *had* to find the answer, had to know whether or not both of these riddles were connected, and if they were, directed solely towards him.

"Good afternoon, Lord Thorne."

"A lie!"

His head shot up, having shouted the answer to the first riddle just as the quiet voice had broken into his thoughts. Lady Hyacinth blinked in evident surprise at his abrupt statement, making Samuel flush with mortification. Setting The London Chronicle down, he rose quickly to his feet. "Lady Hyacinth. Good afternoon."

"Good afternoon." She smiled briefly, though Samuel saw how her gaze flickered towards The London Chronicle. Silently, he prayed that she had not been able to ascertain that he had been working out the answer to the very riddles he had supposedly written himself!

"I thought that you were gone with your mother and sister," he remarked, smiling as warmly as he could and taking in the light flush that touched her cheeks, the swirling questions in her hazel eyes. She was so different in coloring to her sister, with her dark hair where Lady Rose was fair, but Samuel did not think her unbecoming. Truth be told, he was much more inclined toward Lady Hyacinth's company than Lady Rose.

"My sister and mother are gone to take tea with a friend, though I am to take tea with Lady Eve. She and I thought we would follow your lead and come into the bookshop." Her smile was a little uncertain, her gaze pulling from his only to dart back towards him again. "I did want to thank you for the waltz although it was some days ago."

"The waltz?" Still lost in his worries about whether or not she had seen him reading The London Chronicle, it took him a few moments to understand what she was saying. "Oh, yes. The waltz at the ball." The way she was looking at him, the gentle smile on her lips sent Samuel's stomach dipping low. "It was my pleasure, truly." A little surprised that he meant every word, Samuel smiled back at her. The waltz had been nothing sensational, it had merely been a waltz but for her, he had understood that it meant a good deal more.

"I thank you." A pink hint darted into her cheeks. "I shall take my leave of you now. Lady Eve is only just below the stairs and I do not want her to think me lost!"

"I shall accompany you." Picking up The London Chronicle, he saw her glance at it again. "Have you read The London Chronicle's recent publication, Lady Hyacinth?"

Rather than make her way towards the staircase, Lady Hyacinth remained where she was, a strange expression on her face. "I have read some of it, yes."

"And the riddles?" Puffing out his chest just a little, he tried to paste a grin on his face. "I do hope that you enjoyed your time deciphering them."

A sharpness came into her eyes. "I did not need to *decipher* them, Lord Thorne."

This made his grin fix in place. "No?"

"No." She tossed her head and turned away from him. "I perceived the answers in an instant."

Samuel closed his eyes for a second as a crashing wave of embarrassment washed over him. This was now the second time she had made it plain that the riddles were of no difficulty to her and he ought to have remembered that. "I – I must say, Lady Hyacinth, you have the most intelligent mind, I think."

She turned just before reaching the staircase, her eyes a

little narrowed now. "Do you mean to call me a bluestocking?"

"No." He frowned. "But nor do I think that being a bluestocking should be any sort of embarrassment."

This made her eyes widen rather than narrow, a fresh bloom of color in her face.

"I know that it is the consideration of most members in the *ton* that young ladies who adore all manner of learning ought to be ignored and rejected but I do not think so." He spoke truthfully, shrugging his shoulders lightly. "The riddles are for all in the *ton*, not just for the gentleman."

This did not bring about the reaction he had expected. For whatever reason, Lady Hyacinth scowled at him, spun on her heel, and marched down the staircase, making it quite clear by the distance she put between them that she did not want even one more moment of his company.

Whatever did I say?

Frowning, Samuel hesitated before returning to where he had been sitting, his mind returning to the two riddles. The first one's answer was 'a lie' and the second 'deceiver'.

Unfortunately for him, though he did not want to state that the riddles were directed towards him, it appeared, certainly, that they might well be. The riddle writer, whoever it was, had heard that *he* had taken the glory that ought to be theirs and was claiming it for himself.

His lips tugged to one side as his brow furrowed. Who precisely would be writing these riddles? Yes, he had only spoken with Lord Elledge, Lord Jedburgh, Lady Hyacinth, Lady Eve, and Miss Fortescue initially, but given the way Lady Rose had exclaimed today that she knew of his penmanship, Samuel had very little doubt that Miss Fortescue – if not others – had been telling members of the *ton* his supposed 'secret'. Lord Jedburgh was not exactly well known for his quiet nature and Samuel had already been concerned about his penchant for gossip! Closing his eyes, Samuel let out a slow breath, the regret he had felt a short while ago returning, though this time, it came, hand in hand, with guilt.

Just what was he to do?

CHAPTER EIGHT

"Oh, I do not know what to *think* when it comes to Lord Thorne!"

Lady Eve smiled indulgently as Hyacinth walked up and down the drawing room, her whole being burning with what felt like righteous anger.

"One moment, I think him a kind-hearted gentleman who, whilst arrogant, still can show consideration. And then the next, I hear him lying directly to me and I want to shake him by the shoulders and force the truth from him!"

"That is very frustrating indeed, I am sure," Lady Eve answered, calmly. "Though what you have done is all you *can* do, I think." Tipping her head, she lifted one eyebrow. "Unless you wish to tell him the truth."

Hyacinth snorted and shook her head, feeling as if she were wearing holes in the floor given the sheer number of times she had passed back and forth. "I cannot do that."

"Then put your anger into your riddles," Lady Eve suggested. "The last two were very pointed and, given what you told me, it seemed clear to me that he understood them."

This made Hyacinth nod, though she continued to walk. What Lady Eve did not know – and what Hyacinth barely wanted to admit to herself – was that the reason for her frustration was not solely because of the riddles.

They were also because of her own foolish heart.

The night she had danced the waltz with Lord Thorne, she had lost herself completely. Being in his arms, being twirled around the floor with ease as he had smiled down into her eyes... it had made her feel as though she were, in fact, pretty enough to be noticed by a gentleman. It was as if someone had truly *seen* her for the very first time, as though she were someone to be admired and considered, rather than being ignored. Yes, it had taken her great courage to step out as she had done, fear had bitten up and down every part of her frame... but the moment he had taken her into his arms, all of that had broken apart and slithered away, leaving her with a sense of happiness which had been utterly absent from her ever since she had stepped into society again.

And yet, at the very same time, Hyacinth knew that he was a liar, that he had taken on something that was not his to own and was now quite contented with everyone believing it. It was not that she wanted the *beau monde* to look at her with admiration, rather that she simply did not wish for him to steal it for himself without seemingly a second thought.

"He told me that he did not think that a young lady being a bluestocking was anything to be mocked. I thought well of him for that."

"Indeed." Lady Eve sighed quietly and shook her head. "It is a very strange situation, I grant you. Lord Thorne is, as I have told you, prideful and arrogant. And yet, at the very same time, he has shown you personally that he is still an upstanding gentleman, for he has protected you from that despicable Lord Sunderland on two occasions now, has he not?"

Hyacinth nodded and finally made her way to a chair, though she slumped down in it as a sense of tiredness began to wash over her.

"Thereafter, he chose your waltz and that came when he heard Rose teasing you," Lady Eve continued, her reminders only adding to Hyacinth's inner turmoil. "And he has told you that he does not condemn bluestockings! Those things are all commendable, certainly."

"They are."

Lady Eve spread out her hands. "But at the very same time, this gentleman has been telling others that *he* has been writing these riddles and he has done so to gain popularity and admiration, I am sure."

Hyacinth's lips twisted. "That is why I find myself so confused by him. He is not a gentleman who appears to have excellence in his character but also deep failings which are injurious to me personally."

Her friend said nothing, giving Hyacinth the silence she needed to let her thoughts continue to spill out from her mind.

"I do not want to punish him by forcing him, somehow, to admit that he was wrong to say such a thing but neither do I want him to continue to state that he has been writing these! Yes, the riddles can directly speak to him but what hope is there of his repentance? I do not think that a gentleman who has such pride within him will do anything other than seek that out!"

"You mean to say that you do not believe anything will change?" Lady Eve settled her hands in her lap as Hyacinth nodded. "It may, however." Her eyes darted towards

Hyacinth and then pulled away again. "You are continuing to spend time in his company and that can only be a good thing. Somehow, you will be able to catch him out. You are *clever* with words and you will be able to find a way to bring out the truth from him. Even if he does not admit it to society, he will admit it to you and that will bring you victory, will it not?"

Hearing the confidence her friend had in her brought tears to Hyacinth's eyes. "You think that I could do such a thing? Truly?"

"I do."

Hyacinth considered this, her eyes closing as she brought a sense of calmness back to her mind. The truth was, she wanted nothing more than to hear Lord Thorne admit to her that he was wrong, that he *had* lied and taken something that was not his. She did not need the *ton* to hear it, she only wanted the truth for herself.

"Then you must be fixed upon your intentions," Lady Eve continued, speaking firmly now. "Write your next riddles. Make them directly for him, making it clear that you know what he has done and that you are angry at his deceit. Then, go to speak with him. Talk about the riddles and the answers. Try to find a way to catch him out."

A specific worry began to gnaw at Hyacinth's mind. Though she fully agreed with what Lady Eve had suggested, her fear was that, as she spent more time with Lord Thorne, she would find herself drawn to him. She could not confess that to Lady Eve for fear that her friend would think her the most ridiculous creature in all of London and, in this moment, Hyacinth feared that she might truly be so!

"Hyacinth?"

"Mmm?" Hyacinth lifted her head and looked back at

her friend, seeing the enquiring look on her face. "Yes, you are quite right. I can do all those things. I want to hear the truth from his lips and that is the *only* thing that matters." Silently demanding that she have no such foolishness about Lord Thorne any longer, Hyacinth lifted her chin as a steadiness returned to her. "And I shall get it from him, one way or the other."

"I can see Lord Thorne over there."

A coldness rifled up Hyacinth's spine. "Yes, Mama. I can see him also."

"You should go to speak with him. I can still observe you from where I am."

Hyacinth turned to look into her mother's face. "Mama, I am aware that you know I waltzed with him but that does not mean anything. He was only showing me a kindness."

Ice poured into her mother's expression. "And I will not permit you to retreat into the wallflower that I know you desperately wish to be! You have not done as well as I expected nor as I demanded and yet, even now when I tell you to go and speak to a gentleman who has shown you a *miniscule* amount of interest, you refuse?" Her mother's hand pressed hard onto Hyacinth's shoulder, making her wince as she battled hot tears over her mother's cruel words.

"I did not refuse, I – "

"Rose has a good many gentlemen vying for her attention and though I expected that from her, given her beauty. You, on the other hand, ought to be pursuing every gentleman who so much as gives you a second look! There are not many, as you well know, and you cannot be so particular, Hyacinth." Her eyes narrowed all the more. "Your father always retreats to the card room on these occasions and leaves *me* to the responsibilities that both you and your sister bring and you *shall* not let me down. Go. Now."

There was no choice but for Hyacinth to do as her mother demanded. What made things all the worse for her was that the words her mother had spoken had hit her so hard, they had sent sharp tears into her eyes and now, she was on the verge of bursting into sobs. The push of her mother's hand against her shoulder forced her steps and though Hyacinth made her way forward, her vision began to blur and she could not fully see where she was going.

"Lady Hyacinth, are you quite all right?"

Closing her eyes tightly, Hyacinth took in a breath, fearing that her composure was quite lost from her. "I am, yes."

"You do not look to be all right."

Managing to open her eyes and relieved that no tears fell, Hyacinth looked up into Lord Elledge's kind face. "Oh, Lord Elledge, good evening." Her lip wobbled. "Forgive me, it is only that I... " She trailed off, not certain what to say, feeling her emotions building. Lord Elledge had such a kind face and she had thought him very amiable before and her heart did ache so very terribly. "There can be a good deal of expectation on a young lady at evenings such as this, I suppose." Her smile managed to return. "That is all."

"Ah." Lord Elledge nodded. "Were my wife here, then I am certain she would sympathize." His smile was gentle. "Is there anything that I can do? Might you wish to dance?"

Hyacinth took her dance card from her wrist." It would certainly lessen the expectation upon me, if I were to have a few dances on my card."

He nodded and took it from her. "Then I shall be glad to oblige. And here, let me take you to Lord Thorne, he has danced before and I am sure he will do so again." A small frown darted between his eyebrows. "Though I confess, he is not quite himself this evening so he may not desire dancing."

"Not himself?" Hyacinth, managing to gather herself a little more now that she had the kindness of Lord Elledge offered her, took his proffered arm. "In what way?"

"Oh, I do not know." Lord Elledge frowned, glancing towards her. "I am speaking out of turn, mayhap, but I think that our conversation is making you feel a little better and thus, I shall continue." He smiled as she looked away, a little embarrassed to have been so obviously upset. "I cannot tell you with any confidence as to what is concerning Lord Thorne, the only thing I know is that now the *ton* know that he is supposedly the writer of these riddles, it has not brought him any joy. Instead, he appears to be a little more troubled."

"Supposedly?" The word was out of Hyacinth's mouth before she even had time to think. When Lord Elledge's face turned red, Hyacinth's eyebrows lifted gently. It was clear to her that Lord Elledge did not entirely believe Lord Thorne's claim. And that was interesting indeed.

"Forgive my foolishness." Lord Elledge slid a glance towards her. "I ought not to have spoken so."

Hyacinth smiled in what she hoped was an encouraging manner. "But of course."

"Please do not say such a thing to others, especially to Lord Thorne. I do not want to upset him."

"I quite understand," Hyacinth answered. "Though I know for certain that you are not the only one who is a little unsure as to whether such a claim is the truth."

This made Lord Elledge's eyes widen.

"Though I shall trust *you* not to say anything in that

regard also," Hyacinth smiled as Lord Elledge began to chuckle. "We are in each other's confidence now, yes?"

The gentleman's smile grew all the more. "Yes indeed, Lady Hyacinth. It seems as though we are." There was nothing more that could be said between them, for Lord Elledge had brought her to speak with Lord Thorne and the other companions standing near him which, Hyacinth knew, would bring her mother a good deal of relief. She glanced over her shoulder to see her mother nodding in her direction, her eyes narrowed and fixed on Hyacinth's back.

That made Hyacinth's stomach twist with nervousness, fully aware of just what her mother expected – and how little she would be able to fulfill it. To dance every dance was a thought that both frightened Hyacinth and filled her with doubt, for she would never be able to garner that many acquaintances and did not have the confidence to make such connections in the way Rose did! All Rose had to do was walk into the ballroom, smile, and in an instant, she would have at least three dances already taken.

Hyacinth had to fight for even one and even that made her deeply uncomfortable.

"I was just saying to Lady Hyacinth that you are a little altered this evening."

Hyacinth forced her gaze back to Lord Thorne who, much to her surprise, did not attempt even to deny what his friend had said. Just as usual, his expression betrayed all that he was feeling and it was clear to Hyacinth's eyes that he was distinctly out of sorts. His eyebrows were heavy, his gaze flicking back and forth from one face to the next and his jaw was tight. With lifted shoulders, he folded his arms over his chest and then shrugged.

"I am fatigued, that is all."

"Though you shall still dance with Lady Hyacinth, I am

sure." Lord Elledge, who had not yet returned Hyacinth's dance card, handed it directly to Lord Thorne, giving him no opportunity to refuse. "There is an expectation on young ladies, as I am sure you can understand, and I think it our duty to aid that expectation."

The Marquess did not agree nor disagree but took the card from Lord Elledge with a grunt. He scribbled his name and then returned it to Hyacinth with a nod, making no attempt at conversation.

"I was just speaking to Lord Elledge of the riddles," Hyacinth began, recalling what Lady Eve had told her to do. "The most recent one I found most intriguing! I must ask you, is there something that you are trying to say to the *ton*?"

Lord Thorne shifted on his feet. "I do not know what you mean."

"Well," Hyacinth continued, warming to the subject now, "the previous two riddles spoke of lies and deceiving, and then the answer to this most recent riddle was the proverb, 'be sure your sins will find you out' which, of course, was very cleverly written." She tilted her head, watching him carefully. "I suppose I wondered if these riddles were meant to be on a specific subject, hold a message, or if they were simply what you have come up with?"

Lord Thorne looked away, his jaw still tight. "It was entirely by chance that the answer to the riddles were related," he said, sounding frustrated and irritated. "I did not mean them to be in any way connected."

"I see." Hyacinth watched Lord Thorne, wondering what it was that troubled him so. As she had noted before, he was not a gentleman able to hide his emotions from anyone. He was only capable of displaying them right across his face and in his manner. "I do wonder if you might be able to tell me what it is that you do to come up with these riddles, Lord Thorne? I should very much like to know the way in which your mind bends these words and phrases together to create something so mysterious!"

"Why do you not take a turn about the ballroom and explain yourself?" Lord Elledge exclaimed, throwing Hyacinth a smile, though Hyacinth herself found the idea a little worrying, her increasing confidence suddenly thrown asunder. "Lord Thorne will never tell you this himself, Lady Hyacinth, but he is a gentleman very much inclined towards good company... and by that, I mean company that enjoys him hearing speaking about himself!"

Lord Thorne scowled, dropped his hands to his sides but did not say anything in response.

"I shall accompany you, if you wish?" Lord Elledge suggested, glancing behind him to where Hyacinth's mother stood. "And I am sure that Lady Coatbridge will follow also." He leaned towards Hyacinth, murmuring out of the corner of his mouth. "Continue with your questions, Lady Hyacinth. Though you must tell me if you discover the truth!"

"What is it that you are saying?" Lord Thorne sounded irritated but Lord Elledge only smiled.

"Nothing in the least. Now, are you to walk?"

Hyacinth's heart slammed hard against her chest as Lord Thorne finally turned his gaze towards her. He had not much choice in the matter, she realized, for to refuse would be to behave very poorly indeed. She did not know whether or not she wished to walk with him, for though she was doing what Lord Elledge had suggested, there was that niggling sensation in her heart that she simply could not get rid of.

The sensation of a small and yet growing interest in Lord Thorne.

"Very well." Lord Thorne offered Hyacinth his arm and, after only a brief hesitation, she accepted it. "Though we cannot be long. I have to dance with Miss Saxton very soon."

Without a word, though she caught a satisfied smile on Lord Elledge's face, Hyacinth took Lord Thorne's arm and began to walk. Neither of them said a word for some minutes, to the point that Hyacinth began to fear that she would soon be returned to her mother without having had any conversation with the Marquess at all!

"Expectation."

A little confused, Hyacinth glanced up at him, seeing the shadows still filling his expression. "I beg your pardon?"

"Lord Elledge spoke of expectation and what it is to sit upon a young lady's shoulders." Lord Thorne spoke a little more quietly now, though he did not look at her. "Might I enquire what expectation it is that troubles you?"

This was *not* the way the conversation had been meant to go and Hyacinth began to stumble over her words. "Well, yes. The reason is... what I mean to say is that when Lord Elledge came upon me, I was... " Her eyes closed briefly as she tried to return her mind to one thought at a time. "I am sure that you need not hear my explanations, Lord Thorne."

"And what if I should like to?"

Surprised, Hyacinth looked up at him and this time, he held her gaze.

"I am quite genuine, Lady Hyacinth."

Again came the wall of confusion that surrounded Hyacinth's mind. Lord Thorne was proving himself to be a very considerate gentleman in this conversation but she, however, was meant to be speaking with him to force him to reveal the truth about the riddles. And yet, her heart *wanted* to share with him, wanted to tell him the truth about her present difficulties.

"That is very kind of you, Lord Thorne." Confused by her reaction and her desires, Hyacinth hesitated. "I am afraid that such a thing must be kept entirely to myself."

"And why is that?" Lord Thorne's eyebrows rose high. "You do not think that I will gossip about whatever you say to me, do you?"

Hyacinth said nothing, catching the edge of her lip.

"I am not inclined towards gossip, Lady Hyacinth. That is Lord Jedburgh's forte and I am not at all contented with all that the *ton* enjoys. I do not like that rumors and whispers spread all through London for I have seen it cause a good deal of difficulty. You can trust me, I assure you."

A sudden idea came to Hyacinth's mind. "Then I shall tell you, Lord Thorne. But only if you swear you shall tell me something of your own thereafter. That way, I can be assured that you will not whisper about what I have told you."

This made Lord Thorne frown.

"Though there is no need to promise me such a thing if you do not desire to do so," Hyacinth continued, quickly. "We can simply continue as we are."

"Hmm." Lord Thorne's steps slowed and Hyacinth was grateful that they remained close to the perimeter of the ballroom, for it meant that fewer people were noticing them and thus, the conversation could continue without interruption. As she waited for his decision, Hyacinth considered just how quickly her nervousness had fled, how the worries she had endured about walking arm in arm with Lord Thorne had hurried away the more they had walked together. She would not say that she was entirely comfortable in his company but there was a certain easiness about being with him that was growing steadily.

"Very well, Lady Hyacinth. I shall do as you ask." Lord Thorne offered her brief though not a warm smile. "If you tell me something that I promise not to share, then I shall tell you the very same."

Hyacinth smiled back at him. "So I shall tell you what is troubling me and you shall tell me what is troubling you." Seeing him open his mouth to protest that this was not what he had meant to agree to, she spoke quickly so that he could not step away from it. "The expectation from my mother is what I find particularly difficult, Lord Thorne." Her shoulders lowered as a small sadness began to push its way back toward her heart. "You must know, as Lord Elledge said, that every young lady has expectations placed upon her and I am one of those young ladies. Though, of course, the weight is greater on my shoulders than on my sister's."

"Why is it greater?"

Something like a thousand butterflies began to flutter their wings in her stomach. Should she be honest? Yes, she reasoned, for it was not as though Lord Thorne would not be aware of the distinction between herself and her sister. "Rose is not plain as I am. She has greater poise and confidence and enjoys spending time in society whereas I find it a little more difficult."

At this, Lord Thorne stopped dead and turned to face Hyacinth, her hand slipping from his arm. His eyes were a little wider than before, searching her face as if the answer she had given him was a little displeasing. Hyacinth opened her mouth to say something more, only to close it again, feeling her mouth growing dry.

"My dear Lady Hyacinth, I am utterly astonished!"

Hyacinth blinked, not only astonished at just how he had spoken to her but also at the fervency of his words.

"You cannot truly find society difficult, as you have said. You have always appeared quite contented within it!" His eyebrows lifted. "And you are certainly not without poise and confidence, certainly not to my eyes at least! And I will not state that you are plain for that is not only rude but entirely untrue. You have a beauty, Lady Hyacinth, that is entirely your own."

Hyacinth was completely overwhelmed. Lord Thorne was speaking frankly and with evident genuineness, leaving her lost for words. All thought of having him tell her the truth about the riddles flew from her mind as she gazed into his eyes, seeing a steadiness there that told her that he was speaking the truth and *only* the truth.

No gentleman had ever said such words to her before. No gentleman had ever stated to her that she was beautiful in her own way, not even her mother nor her father had said such kind words to her. And yet here was this gentleman, telling her something that she had never expected and crushing her heart with joy.

Lord Thorne dropped his eyes. "I have spoken too fervently, I fear."

"No, no. Not at all." Hyacinth's voice was rasping now, her heart ablaze. "You cannot know just how much your words mean, Lord Thorne. Though," she continued, trying to smile despite the frantic way her heart was beating, "I confess to you the truth – I *do* find and have always found society difficult to be a part of. That is why Lord Sunderland was able to approach me as he did that first evening; because I was standing alone, away from everyone else and even away from my sister!"

"I would never have suspected that," Lord Thorne told

her, his frown lifting for the first time since she had stepped into his company. "You have always appeared confident. Yes, you stood alone when Lord Sunderland approached but I thought nothing of it, truth be told. I was more concerned with what my friend was to do or say."

Hyacinth put one hand to her heart. "Thank you for such considerate words, Lord Thorne. I do not think I can express how much they have brought comfort to my heart."

He smiled and for some moments, Hyacinth lost herself in his eyes. When he smiled with warmth, his entire expression and demeanor changed completely, to the point that there was not even a single flickering shadow lingering there any longer.

"I was to tell you what troubled me also, was I not?"

Pulling herself out of the slight daze, Hyacinth tried to remember what it was that they had previously discussed. "Yes, that is so." Remembering that she was trying to have him confess the truth about the riddles, she drew herself up and nodded, trying to remind herself just how much of a liar and deceiver Lord Thorne really was. "So what has been weighing heavily on *your* mind this evening, Lord Thorne? What has you in such a disagreeable frame?"

The edges of his mouth quirked. "I am in a disagreeable frame, am I not?" A wry chuckle pulled from him. "I cannot hide it from anyone, it seems!"

"No, you cannot." When his gaze pulled quickly to her, Hyacinth flushed but continued to speak, choosing to be honest with him. "You are a gentleman who, I think, is unable to hide what he feels from his expression. Though mayhap, if you share your troubles, you might find them a little relieved."

The smile on the Marquess' face softened. "I suppose that is true. Very well, Lady Hyacinth, I shall tell you."

With a look away, he took in a breath and then released it. "I am caught up in a matter which I now find myself regretting." His brows knotted together. "That did not come out clearly. It is not that the matter itself is regretful, rather that I regret my actions within it." Glancing towards her, he lifted his shoulders lightly. "Does that makes sense to you?"

She nodded slowly, a little surprised to hear those words from him.

"I have behaved foolishly and I know very well *why* I did so, but it does not justify it," he continued, looking away from her again as they began to meander slowly around the room again, uninterrupted by anyone. "That is what disturbs me. I should very much like to remove myself from this present circumstance but I cannot."

"Cannot?" Hyacinth tried to hide her confusion, thinking to herself that all the Marquess needed to do was tell the *ton* that he had made the story up, and then all his regrets would fade. "Why is that?"

A hint of red darted across Lord Thorne's cheeks. "Because I am quite prideful, Lady Hyacinth," he answered, astonishing her all the more with his honesty. "That is the truth of it. So I am quite stuck, you see, and there can be no hope of redemption either."

"No?" Both a little frustrated with herself that she had no feelings of anger or upset towards this gentleman, this very one who had stolen her riddles from her, Hyacinth could not help but settle her hand on his for only a moment, seeing his eyes swing around to hers at once. "I do not think that there is anything above redemption, Lord Throne."

He smiled at her and Hyacinth's heart betrayed her utterly in the way that it leapt up. "No? Not even pride?"

"No," she answered, her voice gentle despite her own regret at her actions and feelings. "Not even that."

CHAPTER NINE

What is happening to me?

Samuel scowled at his own reflection before turning on his heel and storming down the staircase towards the waiting carriage. It was all becoming not only upsetting but also confusing, for he had never had any intention of involving his heart in *any* matters when it came to the London Season, only to begin to find himself now thinking solely of Lady Hyacinth!

And I was much too open with her also, he told himself, still scowling. *Why ever did I think it was wise to speak to her as honestly as I did?*

It had been foolish of him to do so for all it had done was make him think of her all the more – and in much more pleasant terms! He had been quite shocked to hear her speak of herself in comparison to her sister, wondering to himself if that was truly what she believed or if it was something that had been said to her so often, she now believed it. That had brought pain to his heart, telling him that, whether he wished it or not, the lady *had* caught his attention.

Sitting back in the carriage, Samuel closed his eyes and sighed aloud. The most recent riddle in The London Chronicle, the one published and handed out this very morning, had taken him some time to discern. Once the answer had come to him, he had winced visibly, relieved that no one else had been present to see it, else they might have realized that the answer had been, yet again, directed towards him.

"A crown I wear, but my throne is naught but lies," he muttered, the words of the riddle having been almost melded into his mind. "I stand tall with my head held high, yet the shadows of fear flicker in my mind. I preen and boast, a peacock in all its glory, yet this one flaw is all that defines me."

Closing his eyes, Samuel's chest tightened as he fought to take calming breaths. Whoever the riddle writer was, it was clear that they knew of him – but his search for who it could be had thus far, brought him nothing. He had not even the smallest idea as to where to look, for it could be any person in the *ton*! It was not as though the trait of arrogance was something that Samuel had hidden from any one of his friends or acquaintances. Indeed, it was, no doubt, something that many in the *ton* were well aware of, for he had never taken any trouble to try and hide it. It was something that he had never truly considered to be concerning... and yet now, seeing his pride clearly, Samuel felt himself a little ashamed.

It was a most discomfiting feeling.

"Ah, you are come at last! I thought I would have to send a servant to your townhouse to make sure you were still to join me here!"

Samuel jumped quickly down from the carriage,

choosing not to tell Lord Elledge of his many thoughts. "My apologies. I am here at Hyde Park all the same."

"And it is already filled with a good many acquaintances, just as you hoped," came the reply. "Come, then, let us begin our walk."

Falling into step beside his friend, Samuel did not do anything to try and improve the silence that came swiftly between them. What was frustrating to him now was that his thoughts seemed to center on Lady Hyacinth, wondering if she would be present in Hyde Park and if he could speak with her.

Though what he would say and for what purpose he wanted her company, Samuel could not think.

"I must ask you, my friend... are you well?"

Hearing Lord Elledge's voice as though it came from a short distance away, Samuel blinked quickly and then glanced towards him. "Of course I am. Why do you ask?"

His friend did not immediately answer and as Samuel looked back at him again, saw the lines forming on Lord Elledge's forehead.

"You are not yourself these last few days," Lord Elledge said, slowly. "I am sorry if there is something troubling you."

Samuel opened his mouth to state that there was nothing wrong, only to frown. Dare he tell Lord Elledge the truth? Dare he state that yes, the problem was his own foolishness in claiming the riddles to be his own?

"I know that there is something," Lord Elledge continued, all the more quietly now. "Please, my friend, do share it. Let there be understanding between us so that I might be of aid to you in some way! It displeases me to see you so concerned."

Samuel's lips twisted. "It seems that I am a gentleman

unable to keep all that I think and feel from my face, is that not so?"

Looking a little surprised, Lord Elledge nodded. "Yes, that is so. Why, who told you?"

"Lady Hyacinth."

Understanding crossed Lord Elledge's face.

"Though I do not think that I could change that about myself, even if I were to try very hard indeed."

Lord Elledge chuckled ruefully. "No, indeed not." He looked towards Samuel again as they continued to walk through the park, not stopping to speak to anyone. "So are you going to tell me the truth? Tell me what it is that upsets you so much?"

With worry growing in his heart, Samuel bit the edge of his lip, wondering. Clearly, Lord Elledge had already noticed the difference in Samuel's character these last few days and Samuel did not want to make things any worse, and nor did he want the *beau monde* to notice it either! But nor could he bring himself to tell Lord Elledge the truth about the riddles, for that would, no doubt, bring his condemnation and possibly the ending of their friendship.

"I think I am beginning to care for a young lady," he blurted out before he could stop himself. "That is all."

In an instant, Lord Elledge stopped dead and Samuel stumbled in his attempt to then not only stop walking but turn to join his friend. Though he regained his composure quickly enough, it felt as though his face were alight and as he scowled at Lord Elledge, Samuel's heart began to berate him for speaking so foolishly and without consideration.

"You care for a young lady?" Lord Elledge hissed, for which Samuel was very grateful given that the number of gentlemen and ladies in the park was growing quickly. "Truly?"

"I do not want to, however," Samuel answered, refusing to respond to his friend's latter question. "That is why I have been so lost in thought, you understand. I must *rid* myself of this!"

Lord Elledge blinked, his eyes widening. "Rid yourself of your affection for this lady, whoever she may be?"

Samuel nodded. "Yes. Precisely."

"But... but why?"

"Because I have no need of it!" Samuel threw up his hands, his frustration with himself beginning to pour out. "I do not want to have any sort of feelings for any young lady, for my intention has always been to wed when *I* decide, and to a young lady of the very highest standing."

Lord Elledge's lip curved. "But you cannot simply throw this away, Thorne! If you have an affection for a young lady, it will do you no good to attempt to rid yourself of it! You say that you have come to care for her, but do you truly think that simply by desire alone you will be able to rid yourself of such feelings?"

Samuel wanted to say yes, he was sure he could do so, but his heart immediately told him otherwise.

"Why do you not open yourself up to the idea of matrimony?" his friend asked, as a tremor ran through Samuel, reminding him of just how little he desired that. "I can promise you that marrying a young lady whom you have come to care about is a *much* better prospect than wedding a young lady that you do not know in the least! A young lady's standing might be quite excellent but her character lacking severely and then what sort of marriage would you have?"

A tightness ran into Samuel's jaw.

"You are fleeing from what might be an excellent notion," Lord Elledge finished, speaking with firmness now.

"And you are doing so only because you are being foolish. Mayhap also because you are frightened."

That final words made Samuel's blood boil. "I am not frightened of anything!" he exclaimed, though his friend quickly shushed him so that he would not grasp the attention of others in the park. "Not in the least! It is certainly not because of fear that I push these things away! It is simply because I have no desire to marry! I have every intention of enjoying the next few years of the Season alone. I have to do my duty at some point, yes, but that does not need to be now."

Lord Elledge, rather than responding fiercely, took a step closer and put one hand on Samuel's shoulder, his eyes boring into him and making him feel a little unsettled. "Your heart ought to be your guide, my friend. To pursue anything other than that will only lead to pain and frustration with yourself... and, mayhap, with some regret."

Those words sliced through Samuel's mind with a fierceness that caused him to catch his breath. It was the very word he had used to express himself to Lady Hyacinth only a day ago and now, it was being repeated back to him by his friend. He already had a great deal of regret over his foolishness when it came to the riddles, did he truly want to be burdened with more?

"I have already resolved not to marry until I have no other choice but to do so," he muttered, though Lord Elledge rolled his eyes and snorted. "That means that whatever it is that I feel at present for this young lady will simply have to either be borne or forgotten. I am quite determined."

"Then you shall miss out on what is one of the greatest joys known to man," came the swift reply, though Samuel did his utmost not to let the words penetrate his mind. "You have laughed at me before, I am well aware, but that is because you have no experience of what it is I speak of, of what I have *experienced*."

Samuel only looked at him.

"Imagine your feelings as they are at present, suddenly multiplied into a thousand times their strength." Lord Elledge began to gesticulate, making Samuel look away for fear that the fervency of his friend's words would take a hold of him. "And then imagine that all you feel is reciprocated, so that when you have your arms around her, you know full well that her heart is just as filled with love as yours."

"Ah, but that is where you are quite wrong!" Samuel answered, the words coming quickly now as he spied a defense. "I have no certainty that Lady – that is to say, the lady that I might have an interest in – has any thought of returning my feelings! She might have no interest in me whatsoever and what happens then? I will find myself without hope and joy, for my feelings will not be returned and all of my happiness will be shattered."

This made Lord Elledge frown. "You say such things in the hope of dissuading me from convincing you to pursue whatever it is you feel," he said, clearly seeing right through all that Samuel had said. "But I shall not be. As I have told you before, I married without having a single thought of affection. But now it is the only thing that fills my heart and my life – and my wife returns it all." He leaned closer, his eyes sharpening on Samuel's. "You could have the very same."

Samuel's heart lurched with a fierce, fresh hope but Samuel put an end to it the very next second, bringing it tumbling down. "I do not want it," he said, clearly, his heart quickly thundering furiously at the lie he had told. "I am quite determined to rid myself of these ridiculous feelings and am sure I will be able to set them aside without any particular difficulty." He took in a breath. "Come now, enough conversation about me. I see some young ladies over there that could do with our company!" He made to stride away towards them, only for Lord Elledge to catch his arm.

When Samuel looked back at him, Lord Elledge was frowning hard.

"Pray do not tell me that you intend to try and forget your feelings simply by being in company with other young ladies, for I can assure you that it will not work."

With a snort, Samuel shrugged and Lord Elledge's hand fell from his arm. "Not in the least," he answered, lying for what was now the second time in quick succession. "Come now, my friend. Let us go and enjoy good company simply for what it is."

"Lord Elledge, Lord Thorne!" One of the young ladies greeted them both with shining eyes, the other young ladies ending their conversation quickly so they might speak with them both. "How wonderful to have you join us."

"I did see your most recent riddle in The London Chronicle this morning," said another, as Samuel's stomach cramped suddenly. "It was *very* good, and I had to ask my mother for her assistance to find the answer!" She giggled and nudged her friend, who flushed quickly, perhaps aware of Samuel's eyes on them both. "My mother told me that it was a reminder that such a trait is not at all desirable when it comes to pursuing gentlemen!"

Lord Elledge smiled indulgently and spoke before Samuel had the chance to do so. "I have not yet seen this riddle," he said, glancing towards Samuel with something in his expression that Samuel could not quite make out. "Might I ask what the answer was?"

"Arrogance," Samuel answered before any of the ladies could do so, seeing the gleam that came into Lord Elledge's eyes. "It was not a particularly difficult one, I think."

This made two of the ladies gasp with another laughing softly.

"Goodness, Lord Thorne, you must think us quite foolish if you say that one was not of any particular difficulty, especially when Lady Samantha has told you that she had to ask her mother for her aid!"

Heat tore into Samuel's face. "That is not at all what I meant."

"It does not matter, please!" Lady Samantha stepped closer, putting one hand on his arm for a brief moment. "*Do* tell us more about these riddles! I should very much like to know how you come up with them."

Out of the corner of his eye, Samuel spotted movement to his left. Turning his head, he looked straight into the eyes of Lady Hyacinth and, in that moment, it felt as though his heart plunged to his feet and then threw itself back up to his chest again. Looking away sharply, he caught Lord Elledge's gaze, flicking first to Lady Hyacinth and then to Samuel, as if he somehow knew precisely that *she* had been the one that Samuel had been speaking of.

Darkness swam into Samuel's mind and, angry with himself for his feelings and his inability to quash them, he turned bodily away from her and instead, spoke warmly to Lady Samantha.

"Well, I can certainly tell you a little but I cannot give too much away, for fear that one of you will be able to do the same and then will replace my work in The London Chronicle!"

The ladies laughed but the sound brought no joy to Samuel's heart. He smiled, but the sound dulled him rather than invigorated him. At the very same time, he caught how Lord Elledge frowned, perhaps aware of what Samuel was doing.

But it was much too late for any change in direction. He was caught up in conversation now, having to speak lie upon lie as he pretended that, yet again, he had been the one who had been writing the riddles, the one sitting at his desk for many an hour as he fought to find a way to twist words around themselves.

All the while, his heart tugged towards Lady Hyacinth and, with every moment, Samuel had to put a good deal of energy into ignoring her completely.

CHAPTER TEN

Two weeks later.

"Might I ask you something?"

Hyacinth nodded as she and Lady Eve sat together on a picnic blanket, Lord Wiltshire standing a short distance away, speaking with another gentleman.

"Are you taken with Lord Thorne?"

The question so astonished Hyacinth that she sat up straight and looked back at Lady Eve, her mouth agape.

Her friend chuckled. "You need not look so astonished. The only reason I ask is because I have noticed just how much time you have spent in his company these last two weeks."

Hyacinth swallowed hard. "That is only because I have been doing as you suggested!" she exclaimed, as Lady Eve's smile grew. "I told you that there was a growing connection between us, but that thus far, I have been unable to have him say anything about the riddles!"

Lady Eve tilted her head. "You have spoken of them?"

Hyacinth nodded, praying that Lady Eve would not ask her any more questions about the present situation and her feelings as regarded Lord Thorne. For the last fortnight, she had been doing nothing but struggling and fighting against her foolish heart which, no matter what she did, never seemed to recall just how much difficulty he had caused her, nor how many lies he had told. Instead, it pulled her towards him, reminding her of his kindness to her, his consideration, and his sweet words which told her that she was just as significant as her sister.

"Your riddles have been very pointed of late also," Lady Eve continued, with a tug of her lips in one direction. "You have had all of the *ton* aware that there is a distinct connection between the riddle answers, for I have heard everyone speaking of them! They have all pointed to a deceiver, a manipulator, a master of disguise, of poor traits such as arrogance and pride. But as yet, you have not had him speak to you of any of the answers?"

Hyacinth shook her head, warmth beginning to pull up from her chest into her neck and her face. The last few conversations she had enjoyed with Lord Thorne had not been about the riddles at all. Instead, they had spoken of all manner of things, including their respective families and hobbies that they both enjoyed. She had discovered, much to her surprise, that he spends a good deal of time reading and that in itself had been a shared connection.

"You may have to be a little more direct," Lady Eve said, gently as if she realized just how much of a difficulty this would prove to be for Hyacinth. "The riddles might start speaking of revelation? Of pulling back the curtain to present the truth?"

Swallowing thickly, Hyacinth nodded though she did not instantly agree. The idea was a commendable one for it might force Lord Thorne to act but at the very same time, she found herself a little afraid. Once the truth came out and he realized that *she* was the one who wrote the riddles and that she had directed those words towards him, then what would he think of her? She might hope that he would be ashamed and upset but that would certainly mean the end of their connection, would it not?

And I am not sure that I want that.

"You could simply ask him directly also," Lady Eve continued, as Hyacinth frowned. "You could tell him the truth. It may be that this plan to have him reveal the truth because of the riddle answers has failed. We might now require a direct approach to find the truth."

Closing her eyes, Hyacinth felt her whole body tense and tight, barely able to imagine that conversation without her heart filling with panic.

"Though I have the impression you do not feel comfortable with that notion," Lady Eve said, as Hyacinth threw her a quick glance and attempted to shrug, albeit without any real degree of strength. "What is it, Hyacinth? Why will you not tell me the truth?"

Pressing her lips together, Hyacinth looked down at her clasped hands in her lap, finding it difficult to even look at Lady Eve. "Because I am conflicted, that is why."

"Conflicted over him?"

Hyacinth nodded. "He has shown me a good many kindnesses of late and I have found myself being a little more vulnerable with him than I had ever anticipated. I have spoken of my sister and my mother and he has been ever encouraging. He has danced with me very often and come to make sure that I am in conversation with others and... " She dropped her head a little lower. "Because of him, I have found myself happier in society, more at ease than ever before. My mother does not accuse me of being a wallflower and indeed, appears to be a little more contented with me. Rose keeps her distance, of course, but she has not been snide nor cruel of late."

"I see." Lady Eve held Hyacinth's gaze. "Then you struggle to know what it is that you feel and what you desire."

Hyacinth nodded.

"But you must tell him the truth – or have him tell the truth to you one way or the other," Lady Eve said, kindly. "Even if you have any sort of affection for him, nothing can build between you when there is this *lie* in the middle."

Seeing exactly what her friend was saying, Hyacinth nodded but closed her eyes again, surprised at the heat behind her eyes. She did not want to cry over him, did not want to have any sort of difficulty in this present situation, and yet, the more time she spent in his company, the more troubling it became.

"Shall we take a short walk?"

Hyacinth opened her eyes just to see Lord Wiltshire standing before them both.

"A fine idea, I think!" Lady Eve agreed, though she quickly glanced towards Hyacinth. "You are welcome to join us, though if you wish to remain close to my mother, then I quite understand."

Hyacinth shook her head and rose, thinking to herself that the walk might do her a good deal of good. "I think that would be most beneficial. I thank you." She watched as Lady Eve took her betrothed's arm, seeing the way he smiled at her and noticing just how tender it was. A flare of envy erupted in her heart but Hyacinth extinguished it quickly, glad that her friend had found such happiness. The three of them began to walk together, with Lord Wiltshire promising Lady Eve's mother that they would not be long nor go too far, and Hyacinth took in long, steadying breaths as she went, grateful for the sunshine, the clean air, and the friendship which surrounded her.

And then, she saw him.

"Good afternoon, Lady Hyacinth, Lady Eve, Lord Wiltshire." As soon as he saw her, Lord Thorne made his way towards them directly, a smile settling on his face. "It is a fine afternoon, is it not?"

Happiness flew through Hyacinth in a single moment as she held his gaze, smiling back at him. Some weeks ago, they had been in this very same park and, when he had seen her, Hyacinth had seen him turn away directly. That had sent a wave of pain through her, something she had never expected. Now, however, he had come towards her without hesitation, and that made Hyacinth's heart lift with a fresh sense of delight. The riddles, his lies, and her confusion all disappeared as though it was a cloud blown away by a strong wind and all she could see was him.

"We are just taking a short walk about the park, though I must make sure to stay near to my mother," Lady Eve told Lord Thorne, as Hyacinth forced her gaze away from him in an attempt to quieten her frantically beating heart. "Are you here to enjoy the fashionable hour? It is not yet time but I am sure it will be very busy indeed."

Lord Thorne smiled, his eyes on Hyacinth as he spoke and she, in turn, looked back at him again. "I am here solely for good company, Lady Eve. That is all."

Hyacinth felt herself warm, the edges of her lips curving as she looked towards him. Was he speaking of her? *To* her? She did not know but yet, the strength of her feelings suddenly redoubled itself, leaving her feeling utterly breathless.

"Might you wish to walk with Lady Hyacinth for a short while, so that I might walk with my betrothed?" Lord

Wiltshire winced as Lady Eve frowned up at him. "I am sorry, my dear, and I mean no offense to you, Lady Hyacinth, but I do desire to have as much time alone with my betrothed as I can, even if it is in the middle of the park!"

Hyacinth laughed softly, fully understanding and eager to show that she took no offense in the least. "I quite understand. I do not wish to pull you away from any conversations, Lord Thorne, and am more than contented to return to your mother, Eve so you can – "

"I would be glad to walk with you, Lady Hyacinth, if you would wish for my company?" Lord Thorne smiled, then glanced away as if he were a little uncertain that she would want to accept him. Hyacinth could not help but smile back at him, her heart racing in her chest as she accepted his arm... though a sharp look from Lady Eve pulled her back. She was meant to be speaking to him about the riddles, was she not? Meant to be asking him all about what they might mean, pushing him this way and prodding him gently to have him make a mistake in his answers or, indeed, simply to tell her the truth! Or, if that was met with nothing but failure, she might then consider asking him outright for the truth.

Could she do it?

I do not want to lose the connection we have. I do not want to break it apart.

"You are quiet all of a sudden, Lady Hyacinth." Lord Thorne looked towards her, a slight lift to his eyebrows. "Are you quite all right? You did not have to accept me, you know. I would not have taken in the least bit of offence if you had refused me."

"I think that you would have done," Hyacinth

answered, teasingly. "You would have been most upset that I refused you."

This made a twinkle appear in Lord Thorne's eyes as he grinned back at her. "Yes, I suppose that is so. Though I have made you smile again and speak with me, so that can be no bad thing."

"Indeed you have." Hyacinth leaned into him a little more, only for another glance from Lady Eve to remind her, again, of her true purpose. Her smile faded just a little as she took in a deep breath, trying to think of a way to speak to him about the riddles that would force his hand. "I must ask, Lord Thorne, whether your riddles are ever going to alter from their present state! They are singularly depressing at the moment, though I mean no offense by that."

Lord Thorne's expression darkened in an instant, his eyes darting to hers and then pulling away. "I do not know what you mean."

"I mean that there is no answer that brings joy," she said, trying to keep her voice light. "They have all been either answers of deceit and trickery, or of traits that one ought not to have in oneself! I believe the last one spoke of disguise and shadows, did it not?"

The tightening of Lord Thorne's jaw did not give her the answer that she had hoped.

"I do hope you do not take offense," she said, a little more gently. "All I mean is that it would be different to see an answer to a riddle that spoke of something good."

Lord Thorne lifted his chin. "The riddles are not something that I wish to speak of, Lady Hyacinth."

The coldness in his tone made her eyebrows lift, though a distinctly uncomfortable sensation flooded her at the very same time.

"I am tired of speaking of them," he continued, keeping his eyes away from her, a tension in his frame which she could feel as they walked arm in arm. "It is all that the *ton* ever seems to speak of, all that anyone seems to ask me and I do not want to have any further discussion on the matter, least of all from you."

Hyacinth blinked, feeling as though a hand was squeezing her heart. She did not know in what tone Lord Thorne had meant that last remark but the way in which he had altered after only a brief comment about the riddles had taken her completely by surprise. He had been nothing but smiles and happiness and then, in the very next moment, turned cold and withdrawn.

She did not know what to make of it. Could it be that he had begun to think that *she* was the riddle writer? That her nearness to him was solely to torment him? No, Hyacinth considered, as they walked now in strict silence, that could not be so. Something about the riddles had now so upset him, he did not even want her to mention it! How different that was from the gentleman he *had* been, the one who had seemed to boast in all that he had supposedly done!

Lord Thorne heaved a sigh and then, after another few moments, paused and shook his head. "Lady Hyacinth, I am sorry. I spoke harshly to you just now and I ought not to have done." His other hand reached across to press her fingers as they walked, sending a fleeting flame of fire up her arm. "I do hope that you can forgive me."

"Of course." Hyacinth heard her voice, a little hoarse and uncertain. "You are upset by the riddles, it seems. I confess, I am surprised."

"As you might well be." There was no other explanation given to her from him other than that. There was nothing more said, nothing more expressed to give her any sort of understanding as to why he was so troubled. Instead, he offered her a wan smile and then, after a moment, turned to bring her back to Lady Eve and Lord Wiltshire.

"I think I must take my leave of you all, alas." Dropping his arm, Hyacinth was released from him, that coolness she had felt from him still lingering. "I can see Lord Sunderland near to me and I confess, I feel it my duty to make certain he does not trouble anyone!"

Hyacinth nodded in understanding, well aware that Lord Thorne did truly feel such a way. He had mentioned in passing, on more than one occasion, how little he thought of Lord Sunderland's behavior and how concerned he had been at times for what might occur, had he not intervened. All the same, the way he would not look into her eyes, the way he did not so much as smile at her made Hyacinth's heart twist in her chest. There was something so very altered about him now, and all because she had mentioned the riddles.

Just what could it be?

CHAPTER ELEVEN

Samuel slumped in his chair, looking dully at the glass in his hand. Lord Jedburgh, Lord Sunderland, and Lord Elledge were in conversation all around him. Indeed, Whites was flowing with laughter and all manner of conversation but Samuel could not partake of any of it.

All he could think of was Lady Hyacinth and the hurt in her eyes when he had spoken to her as he did. These last two weeks, he had continually battled his feelings, telling himself over and over and *over* again that he did not want to fall in love with any young lady and had no interest in courtship or marriage, only to see her again and feel his heart betray all of his intentions. There was something about her that made him come alive, made him feel as though every day was filled with sunshine and brightness and good things.

And then he would be reminded of just how foolish he had been, how his pride had got the better of him, and of how poor a fellow he had truly been, and all of it would shatter. It did not matter how he felt, Samuel had told himself, for the lies he had built up had placed a wall between himself and Lady Hyacinth... and if it came tumbling down, he did not know whether their connection would survive or if it would shatter.

"You are melancholy this evening."

Lord Elledge sat down with a contented sigh and smiled in Samuel's direction, though Samuel did not even lift his gaze.

"You have been melancholy very often these last few days," Lord Elledge continued. "I presume that your feelings for Lady Hyacinth have not faded as you hoped?"

That remark caught Samuel's attention. He flung a look towards Lord Elledge but his friend only smiled, tipping his head in a manner that spoke of understanding and sympathy and in seeing it, Samuel felt himself completely without response.

"It was not hard to understand." Stretching out his legs, Lord Elledge crossed them at the ankle. "You deliberately turned away from the lady the last time we saw her at this very park and it was that action which confirmed it for me."

Samuel's jaw tightened. "I did not think I was so very obvious."

"You most certainly are."

With a sigh, Samuel rolled his eyes. "Pray, do not harp on at me about it all. I have no wish to speak of my confusion."

"Then you are still troubled?" Lord Elledge's lips lifted. "I thought that you were quite determined to set these feelings aside! That you would have no difficulty in removing them from yourself!"

Hearing the words he had spoken some weeks ago now repeated back to him made Samuel's heart burn with both embarrassment and frustration. It had *not* been as easy as he had hoped and, indeed, Samuel had practically given up on all attempts to forget the lady. Only that very afternoon, he had made his way from the lady he *had* been speaking with to go and talk with Lady Hyacinth and that was certainly *not* putting her aside from himself!

"Why do you not ask to court her?"

Samuel threw back the rest of his whisky and set the glass down on the table in front of him. "I have already made my thoughts clear on such matters."

"But you can see now that – "

"And it is because I am a fool," Samuel continued, the urge to tell Lord Elledge the truth about the riddles growing within him so steadily, that he felt as though it might explode from his chest if he did not. "I have not been truthful with Lady Hyacinth and nor have I been with you. Or with anyone."

Lord Elledge sat back in his chair and lifted one eyebrow. "This is about the riddles."

Slack-jawed, Samuel stared at his friend who only shrugged lightly. How had Lord Elledge managed to discern that the riddles had *not* been written by him? He had thought he had managed to deceive everyone, only to now realize that one of his closest friends had not been sure enough to trust him! "I – I thought you believed me," he wheezed, clutching at his heart as a fresh weakness washed over him. "I was sure that – "

"That you had deceived me, as well as everyone else?" Lord Elledge's eyebrow fell, sending a shadow into his eyes. "Why did you say such a thing, Thorne? Why pretend so?"

Shame tore through Samuel's being, his face burning, eyes darting away as he clasped and unclasped his hands, sweat trickling down his back.

"And now you feel as though you cannot pursue Lady

Hyacinth when she, as well as the rest of the *ton* believes your lie?" A flash came into Lord Elledge's eyes. "My dear friend, whatever did you think you were doing? I have been very suspicious that the answers to those riddles were so pointed because there was clear anger directed toward you! Because the person who *actually* writes them is upset that you have stolen their glory from them!"

"I know all of this!" Samuel threw up his hands, his face still scarlet. "I have told you that I am ashamed, that I am regretful but what is there for me to do?"

"Tell her the truth! Tell all of us the truth!"

Samuel shook his head. "I cannot. What will become of me then? What will happen to my connection to Lady Hyacinth?"

Lord Elledge shook his head, clear anger in his expression. "You did this because of your pride, did you not? I knew that you did not have the answer to one or two of those riddles and instead of being truthful and admitting to it, you tried to deceive us so that we would not think less of you."

Closing his eyes, Samuel dropped his head.

"What you do not seem to understand, my friend, is that we would have thought all the more of you had you been honest. There would have been no shame in admitting the truth."

"Mayhap not from your perspective but there would certainly have been shame upon my heart all the same."

His friend shook his head. "And do you truly think that this situation is better? That what you now stand in ought to be something worthy of praise?"

Samuel swallowed thickly but said nothing.

"If you truly care for Lady Hyacinth, if you care anything at all for your friends, then you have a duty to make this right, Thorne. Somehow, in some way, you must make it clear to us all that you are *not* the one who has written the riddles."

Before he could think of what to do or what to say, Samuel was on his feet, hurrying out of Whites and away from Lord Elledge. He had not expected his friend to express such anger and yet, at the very same time, it felt almost refreshing. It was a strange relief in telling even one person about his shame though it had not brought him any sort of understanding or sympathy.

Not that I deserve it.

Jaw tight, Samuel strode towards his carriage, climbing in and, as he rested his head back, closing his eyes. His heart was thundering, his whole body still hot and strained; not only from what his friend had said but also from the utter regret which held such a tight grip upon him.

Reaching up, Samuel rapped on the roof. "Home."

The carriage moved almost immediately and Samuel blew out a small breath of relief. At least, in the quiet of his own house, he might have somewhere to think. Though whether he would find any conclusions, he did not know.

"Lord Elledge, my lord."

Samuel looked up from his desk just as his friend came in. "Lord Elledge, I was not expecting you."

"I am well aware of that." His friend sat down but looked directly into Samuel's eyes. "I am come to apologize."

Samuel's eyebrows lifted. "Apologise?"

"I spoke very sharply to you last evening. I ought not to have done."

All the more surprised, Samuel shook his head. "I

would not say that. You had every right to speak as you did. After all, *I* am the one who has been deceitful, have I not? To my mind, there is nothing that you need to apologize for."

At this, Lord Elledge smiled but it did not reach his eyes. "I would disagree but all the same, I am glad that you feel no distance between us."

"I do not." Glancing down at his paper, Samuel gestured to it. "In fact, I have thought of something I must do in an attempt to rectify it all."

Lord Elledge's eyebrows lifted. "Oh?"

Samuel gestured to his paper. "I am writing my own riddle."

This brought confusion to his friend's face.

"I am going to send it to The London Chronicle, in the hope that it will be published." A grimace tugged at Samuel's lips. "It is a good deal more difficult than I had expected, I confess, though that, mayhap, comes from my own sense of arrogance in believing that it would be particularly hard to write."

"I do not understand." Lord Elledge rose to his feet and came around the side of Samuel's desk to look at his work. "What will this riddle do?"

"It will, I hope, tell the real writer that I am sorry for what I have done and that I wish to seek amends." A little concerned, Samuel tapped his fingers on the table. "Though I do not think I can do it in only one riddle. Mayhap I shall have to write two."

Lord Elledge scratched his head. "And you think that this will encourage the real writer to forgive you?"

"I do not know. But I must do *something*," Samuel stated, fully aware that the easy thing to do – to tell the *ton* that he had lied – was something that he very much did not wish to do. "This might make the writer come to speak with me, to hear me say how much I regret my lies. There might then be a way for us to form a path together, so I might absolve myself somehow."

His friend set one hand on Samuel's shoulder. "It does feel to me as though you are trying to escape the difficult thing."

Samuel nodded, looking down at his riddles again. "Yes, I am. I do not want to tell the truth to the *ton*. I do not want them to know of my foolishness for my pride will be severely injured, my standing brought down and I will, no doubt, have very many people mocking me." His stomach lurched at the thought. "though if it comes to it, I suppose I may very well simply have to tell the truth."

"You may have to, yes." Lord Elledge walked away, though he went only to pour a glass of brandy for them both. "The question is, however, will you have the courage to do it?"

CHAPTER TWELVE

Hyacinth blinked. She could not quite believe what she was reading, her mouth going dry as she read the words. There were *four* riddles in The London Chronicle and she was quite certain she had only sent two in, just as she usually did.

Whatever was this?

"Have you seen it?"

Without warning, the door to Hyacinth's drawing room flew open and Lady Eve hurried in, her eyes wide.

"You are reading it now, then? I knew at once that you had not written the other two, especially when I discerned the answers. They have a good deal less complexity than yours, have they not?"

Hyacinth, who had barely glanced at her friend, fixed her eyes to the first riddle again. "I haunt the present, a creation of choices made in the past. Nothing will unmake me, but with time, I may fade." Lifting her gaze to Lady Eve, it took her only a moment to come to the answer. "Regret. This is speaking of regret."

"And the other is an apology," Lady Eve said, pointing to the next. "What am I, this bridge built solely of words spoken between you and I? A bridge that you might break, should you refuse to meet me there. Rope woven with sorrows binds each step, offered to you freely but with no assurance of acceptance."

"Then he is sorry." Hyacinth dropped The London Chronicle onto the chair beside her, surprised to feel heat behind her eyes. "He would not speak to me of the riddles, when we were in the park. Our conversation was brought to a very sharp end and then he stepped away, leaving me feeling quite confused."

Lady Eve smiled gently. "He regrets what he has done then, yes? He is sorry for it, he wishes to apologize."

Nodding slowly, Hyacinth looked down at the paper again but felt her heart twist with a sudden sharp pain. "And while I am grateful for that, it is not as though he has shown any true repentance."

Her friend's eyes searched hers.

"What he ought to be doing is to speak to the *ton* and to make it clear that he was not the one who wrote the riddles after all!" Hyacinth continued, wishing that she did not feel so much for Lord Thorne, to the point that it was becoming all twisted up inside her. "That would show a true repentance, would it not?"

"Yes, I suppose it would," Lady Eve agreed, softly, "but you know as well as I that the gentleman is prideful."

Hyacinth closed her eyes against a sudden rush of tears. "I understand that, I do, but I want him to show, to *prove* that he is willing to put that aside! I am grateful for his attempt at an apology and I truly do appreciate that he is willing to express regret, but that is done only in a way that makes sense to me. It is not public, it is not making amends in the right way."

Lady Eve let out a small sigh. "Indeed. And it must be all the more trying when your heart holds an affection for him."

Hyacinth threw her a look but could not deny it, the look on Lady Eve's face one of sympathy rather than mockery. Much to her dismay, a single tear trickled down her cheek and though she dashed it away quickly, it was not quick enough for Lady Eve not to see it.

"Oh, my dear friend!" Lady Eve quickly took Hyacinth's hand and pressed it. "I did not realize that you were so caught up with it all!"

"It is foolish, is it not?" Hyacinth sniffed, pulling out her handkerchief and dabbing at her eyes before any more tears could fall. "I should not have any feelings for him, given what I know, but the more time I spend in his company, the more desirous I am of it! I am meant to be speaking with him to push him into telling me the truth but I confess that it has been difficult for me to even *remember* to do so! I am aware of just how foolish I am in this, believe me, but I – "

"I do not think you foolish!" Lady Eve squeezed Hyacinth's hand again, her eyes searching Hyacinth's face. "I have seen Lord Thorne's kindness displayed to you, I have seen his consideration and the goodness within him, just as much as I have seen his pride. Truth be told, I am surprised at how much good I have seen in him, for when I first returned to London, I advised you to stay away from him! Now I have seen how much he seeks to defend you – not only you but other young ladies that Lord Sunderland pursues, for example. There is more to his nature than I ever realized and I would not judge you for feeling drawn to him. I can understand it, truly."

Hyacinth nodded and sniffed but looked away, aware of just how torn her heart was.

"You must be feeling quite broken."

"I am." In answer to Lady Eve's statement, Hyacinth looked back at her, aware of just how much she trembled inwardly. "How can it be that I am falling in love with the very gentleman who has been so deceitful? And just what am I to do?"

Her friend frowned and said nothing for a few moments. Thereafter, she nodded in a seeming decisive manner, then smiled. "You must be honest with him. You must tell him what you know *and* what you feel... though mayhap the other way around."

Nothing but shock washed over Hyacinth as she stared back at Lady Eve, who only smiled. "I – I cannot do that."

"You must." It all seemed so very easy for Lady Eve, though Hyacinth shook her head in response. "How else are you to bring an end to this torment? How else are you to find a clear path to walk along? Either you tell him all or you continue in this strange darkness, where you are pulled in two directions. It can only be as simple as that."

Instantly imagining what it was Lord Thorne would say when she told him, Hyacinth trembled visibly. "He will pull away from me."

"And if he does?"

Hyacinth closed her eyes tightly, trying to fight against the fresh wave of tears that threatened.

"Then he was never worth of you," Lady Eve murmured, ever so gently. "You must tell him the truth *or* garner the truth from him, Hyacinth. It is the only way."

Opening her eyes and relieved that no more tears fell, Hyacinth nodded slowly, her heart still in a quandary. She could see the wisdom in what Lady Eve was saying but at the very same time, she wanted to do nothing of the sort, afraid of what would occur if she did.

But I cannot pretend forever, she told herself, her throat tightening. *To continue in this way will bring me nothing but pain and confusion.*

"Tonight," she said, a little hoarsely. "I shall speak to him tonight, at the ball."

Lady Eve nodded, relief in her expression. "Tonight."

"Good evening, Lord Thorne." Hyacinth forced a smile that she did not truly feel, aware of the tension that raked through her as he took her hand and bent over it. "How very pleasant to see you this evening."

"And you." Lord Thorne lifted his gaze to her and smiled. "I am hopeful that your dance card is not yet entirely full, Lady Hyacinth?"

"Full?"

Hyacinth closed her eyes briefly as Rose, who was standing near, let out a bright laugh that Hyacinth knew full well was meant to taste of mockery.

"I do not think that Hyacinth's dance card has ever been full at any ball we have attended, Lord Thorne," she continued, throwing Hyacinth a look that made her wither inwardly. "You need not have any fear there."

Wishing that the floor would open up and swallow her so that she did not have to endure this mortification, Hyacinth did not know where to look, aware of the burning heat in her face. Rose had not spoken in such a way towards her for some time but something about Lord Thorne and his attentions towards Hyacinth was clearly upsetting her.

"Then I must make sure that is not the way of things this evening!" Lord Thorne moved a little closer, sidestepping Rose and instead, coming to stand a little closer to their mother who, up until the very moment he appeared beside her, had been in conversation with another young lady. Hyacinth watched on, thoroughly confused as Lord Thorne bowed to her mother.

"Lady Coatbridge, good evening."

Hyacinth's mother glanced at both of her daughters as Lord Thorne bowed. "Good evening, Lord Thorne."

"I have been informed by Lady Rose that your daughter, Lady Hyacinth, has never had a full dance card at any ball," Lord Thorne continued, throwing a quick smile towards Hyacinth, though it was Rose who turned a shade of scarlet such as Hyacinth had never seen. "I should very much like to make sure that she has every dance taken this evening, Lady Coatbridge. Might I be permitted to take her to meet some of my acquaintances? Gentlemen of excellent repute, I might add!" He turned and pointed over Hyacinth's shoulder. "I shall only just be over there but I will make sure that her dance card is quite filled to the brim by the time we return!"

"Oh, Lord Thorne, how very kind of you."

Hyacinth did not know what to say, hearing her mother continue to gush with delight over Lord Thorne's generosity whilst she did not know whether to feel embarrassed or delighted. Rose hung her head, perhaps aware that her mother would soon speak sharply to her for what she had revealed to Lord Thorne. It was a very kind gesture from him, though at the very same time, she felt a little overwhelmed by his consideration.

Does it mean something more? she found herself

wondering, a sudden flare of hope bursting through her. *Could it be that what I feel is returned?*

That hope died at the very next moment as she recalled all that she had determined to say to him. They were meant to be speaking of the riddles, meant to be telling him the truth about it all and trying to confess her heart at the same time and that meant there could be no certain hope, not when she could not be sure as to how he would respond!

"Come, Lady Hyacinth."

Hyacinth blinked, tugged out of her thoughts as Lord Thorne offered her his arm, a warm smile on his face. "Lord Thorne?"

"We will have your dance card filled in a matter of moments," he promised, "though I have taken the waltz and the quadrille. It is a little selfish, mayhap, to have the first choice but I was the first to come to speak with you!"

The flooding warmth which came from his words made Hyacinth's heart soften all over again, chasing away her fears and her worries in a moment, only for them to rush over her again, as though it was one wave followed by another onto the crashing shore. "You are very kind, Lord Thorne. I did hope that we might be able to speak together, at some point this evening."

"I should like that." Lord Thorne gave her another smile, though Hyacinth did not feel any reassurance at it. "There are some things I should like to share with you, though it can be difficult to have a conversation at a ball!"

"I am attending Lord and Lady Markham's soiree tomorrow evening," Hyacinth replied, seeing a light dart into his eyes. "Mayhap there we might find time to speak together?"

He nodded. "That would be quite perfect, I think."

Hyacinth smiled back at him, choosing, yet again, to push away her fears and instead allow them to fill up all of the spaces that would come with tomorrow's conversation, though quite what he wanted to say, she did not know. This evening, it seemed, she was able to dance and laugh and smile and enjoy all that this ball had to offer her... and it was all because of what Lord Thorne had chosen to do for her and for her alone.

CHAPTER THIRTEEN

Samuel took in a deep breath and set his shoulders, looking all around the room for Lady Hyacinth. After last evening, he had returned home but had not retired, instead choosing to sit down and consider his feelings and what it all might mean.

It had been a somewhat terrifying few hours as he recognized that all that he had once thought and expected of matrimony might be entirely wrong. Lord Elledge's expression and explanation of his marriage left Samuel with a sense of longing rather than a bad taste in his mouth, as it had done before.

And in the center of it all sat Lady Hyacinth.

Samuel's heart was filled with an anxiety that he could not simply push away. It had grown with every minute that he had spent at this soiree, desperate to see her so that he might pull her to one side and tell her what was on his heart. He could not continue as he was, pretending that his feelings held no significance. Instead, he was going to have to be honest with her about it all, about his former thoughts on matrimony, about his feelings at the present moment, and much to his upset, his foolishness as regards the riddles. That had brought a dark cloud to his mind for he feared what her reaction would be when he told her the truth about them but it had to be done. He could not hold a lie between them. The riddles he had placed in The London Chronicle had brought him no response, not thus far anyway, which meant he had no choice but to tell Lady Hyacinth the truth, and, thereafter, everyone else. Whether it would cost him his pride or not, Samuel knew what he had to do – and recognized that it was his own foolishness that had brought him to this point. Everything could change for him in this one evening, though for good or for bad, Samuel did not know.

There she is.

A light smile played about his mouth as he took in the young lady, barely giving a glance to either her sister or to Lord and Lady Coatbridge. Lady Hyacinth had lowered her head just a little whilst Lady Rose lifted her chin and looked all around the room, clearly delighted to be in amongst company.

"Now, who is it that *you* are looking for?"

Samuel wrinkled his nose as Lord Sunderland leaned into him, though it was not out of any sort of friendliness that he did so. "You cannot be so heavily in your cups already, surely?"

"You did not answer my question." Lord Sunderland chuckled, his eyes half closing as he staggered back one step. "Tell me, who is it that you are looking at? I can tell that you were fixed upon some young lady and yet – "

"I am, in fact, wondering if Lord Elledge is yet present, for he was meant to be joining us this evening," Samuel interrupted, having no intention of telling Lord Sunderland anything. "He and I have some matters to discuss."

Lord Sunderland chuckled but it was not a pleasant sound, making Samuel wince inwardly. He pitied the young ladies present this evening, knowing full well that his friend would try and capture the attentions of as many as he could... even though most of the young ladies present would be repulsed by him, Samuel was sure.

"I am determined to find a new flirtation this evening," Lord Sunderland said, with a wide grin. "I have grown tired of Lady Helensburgh."

With a frown, Samuel threw a glance at him. "Lady Helensburgh?"

"It is better that you do not know," Lord Sunderland answered, seeming to try to draw himself up. "Needless to say, she and I have become weary of each other and it is better now for me to find someone new."

"Then go and do so." Samuel, eager to go and speak to Lady Hyacinth, made to step away, only to see Lord Sunderland's beady eyes following after him. With a sigh, he moved away from Lady Hyacinth's direction, forcing his steps towards the door. Fully aware that Lord Sunderland would be watching him, Samuel made his way out into the hallway and then into the music room, thinking that he would stay for only a few short minutes until Lord Sunderland had grown tired of his foolish game and become distracted by something – or someone else.

"Lord Thorne, good evening."

Samuel, seeing Lord Jedburgh and a few other acquaintances, nodded. "Good evening to you all."

"We are speaking of the riddles in The London Chronicle. *Your* hard work, yes?"

Not sure what he ought to say for the desire to say that yes, he *was* responsible was no longer present, Samuel only shrugged.

"You have certainly taken us all by surprise with these last two," came the response from another gentleman. "I thought they were all on the same theme but the answers to these two were very different!"

Samuel frowned, having very little idea as to what the gentlemen were talking about for he had not seen the riddles in The London Chronicle that day. "You were displeased with them?"

"No, no, not in the least!" cried Lord Jedburgh as the other gentlemen all said the same. "What Lord Frederickson means to say is that your previous riddles all had answers on dark or displeasing things, but these two were not so! The first – the answer *truth* – was very well written, I must say, and the second, the one that spoke thankfulness –"

"I took it to mean appreciation," interrupted another, though Lord Thorne kept his gaze pinned to Lord Jedburgh.

"Thankfulness or appreciation, whatever you wish." Lord Jedburgh waved a hand. "Those two answers mean much the same thing but again, they were on a very different *theme* from your previous answers."

"Indeed." Samuel's heart beat hard as he realized that the riddle writer had, yet again, used the riddles to speak to him. The one that said 'appreciation' was, mayhap, expressing thanks for his regret and his desire to apologize, but the other, 'truth'... did that mean that they expected him still to admit the truth to everyone? To urge him to be honest and clear with everyone? Samuel's stomach tied itself in a tight knot as he thought of what might happen should he do so, wishing that he had the courage and the gumption to do what he knew he ought.

"Lord Thorne?"

Samuel cleared his throat and forced a smile. "I am glad that people find the riddles so amusing still." He made to turn on his heel, only for another gentleman to join them, his brow furrowing.

"Lord Thorne, good evening." Lord Elledge's dark expression was directed straight towards Samuel, making his face flush as guilt crashed over him. "You are speaking of the riddles, then?"

Samuel shook his head. "I was just about to take my leave as there is someone that I wish to speak with, rather urgently I might add." He held Lord Elledge's gaze, fully aware now of what he needed to do – and just how little he desired to do it. "Thereafter, I shall come back to speak with you all."

This seemed to pull some of the darkness from Lord Elledge's expression and he nodded, as though he were giving Samuel his mark of approval. Relieved, Samuel excused himself and turned away, going in search of Lady Hyacinth.

Strangely, she was not in the drawing room, where he had last seen her with her mother and disagreeable sister. Frowning, Samuel stepped back into the hallway and meandered slowly through it, stepping back into the music room and, thereafter, into the parlor. She was not there, though as he came out of the parlor, he recognized Lady Coatbridge standing talking to a gentleman, with Lady Rose beside her.

Of Lady Hyacinth, there was no sign.

Worry began to niggle in his heart as he made his way towards them both, thinking it a little surprising that Lady Hyacinth had stepped away. Though, he remembered, if Lady Eve was present then there was every expectation that Lady Hyacinth was standing with her.

Mayhap they have gone into the library.

The door was close to Lady Coatbridge and Samuel pushed it open gently, stepping into a fairly dark room, lit only by a few candles and a small fire in the grate. He frowned, a little surprised that their host had thought to make it so dim, only to hear a quiet cry.

Spinning around, Samuel tried to make out the shadows in the darkness, striding forward toward the far corner of the room.

"What is the meaning of this?" Yanking back the curtain that covered the window, Samuel exposed not only the moonlight that came streaming through but also a gentleman standing directly in front of a lady, practically pinning her to the wall. His shoulders dropped as distaste crawled up his spine. "Sunderland, if you are going to begin a new flirtation, do you not think that you could choose a more private place than this?"

"Thorne!"

The voice that reached him was not that of Lord Sunderland, who appeared now to be leaning against the wall, crushing the lady beneath him. Much to Samuel's horror, he realized that the voice was coming from none other than Lady Hyacinth, the very young lady he had been searching for. Fear tore through him, his heart pounding as he grabbed Lord Sunderland bodily, forcing him out of the way though Lord Sunderland only slumped back against the wall entirely, a lazy grin on his face.

"Lady Hyacinth!" Samuel caught her in his arms as she let out a sob and almost collapsed into him. His heart was pounding with a fury he could not seem to fully grasp, wanting not only to protect Lady Hyacinth but also to grab Lord Sunderland by the collar and shake him until he realized precisely what he had done.

And then, Samuel wanted to plant his fist hard into Lord Sunderland's frame.

"He pulled me into here before I could stop him," Lady Hyacinth whispered, her whole body shuddering as her head went to Samuel's shoulder, his arm about her waist. "I did not realize what he intended until it was too late and there was no one else here. I did not know what to do and he was much too strong for me."

Samuel swallowed hard as anger bit down at him again. Lord Sunderland had stolen her away, intending to have his way with her regardless of what she wanted – and had Lady Hyacinth screamed, then she would, no doubt, have ended up being forced to marry the very scoundrel who had dishonored her in the first place. He closed his eyes, trying to control himself, only for the door to the library to swing open and three other guests to come into the room.

Samuel attempted to disentangle himself from Lady Hyacinth as quickly as he could but it was much too late. The third guest, a lady, stopped dead and stared directly at him, no doubt seeing him a good deal more clearly now thanks to the moonlight.

"What is happening here?" Her voice was filled with interest rather than concern and Samuel, looking to Lady Hyacinth, felt his whole body tense. Lady Hyacinth had dropped her head and he could hear her ragged breathing. Fog began to cloud his mind, realizing precisely what difficulty Lady Hyacinth now stood in. She was here alone with not one but two gentlemen, which meant that, unless he did something, her reputation would be ruined.

"Is that a young lady there with you, Lord Thorne?" The lady in question came closer, clearly recognizing him though Samuel did not know who she was, or mayhap that was only because his mind was a little fuzzy. "And another gentleman with you also? How... interesting."

"Lord Sunderland, at your service, my lady." Lord Sunderland's speech was slurred and as he tried to bow, he staggered forward and collided with a chair. This altercation caught the attention of the other two guests who had, until this moment, been conversing together, and they too came closer. Much to Samuel's horror, the door then permitted a good many other guests, all who came in and immediately came closer, perhaps wondering at all the commotion. Samuel's heart slammed hard into his chest, his breathing quickening with every second. He glanced at Lady Hyacinth, seeing how low she had dropped her head, how rounded her shoulders were as he practically felt her dread and resignation. All Lord Sunderland had to do was open his mouth and she would be bound to him forever, else her reputation would be torn to shreds and she would be left a spinster, shamed and disgraced for the rest of her days.

I cannot let that happen.

"Forgive me, I cannot see you in the gloom." The words seemed to come from a place deep within him, making him sound calm and almost contented, despite the frantic beating of his heart and the fog still clouding his mind.

"It is Lady Venables." The lady tilted her head. "Do you have an explanation for this, Lord Thorne? And who is this young lady with both yourself and Lord Sunderland?" She lifted an eyebrow as some of the other guests came to stand directly beside her, making his mind begin to whirl as all the possibilities laid themselves out before him.

"Lady Venables, good evening." Samuel cleared his throat, put his hands behind his back, and tried to smile. "Lord Sunderland, as you can see, is not in a particularly fit state at present. He is in his cups already and – "

"Are you trying to state that Lord Sunderland is the reason for this young lady's presence?" Lady Venables asked, taking a step closer. "That she followed him in here?"

A small, frightened exclamation came from behind Samuel and he half turned, fully aware that Lady Hyacinth must, at this very moment, be feeling nothing but dread.

"No, no, that is not at *all* what I am saying." A little afraid that he was making the situation worse, Samuel took in a deep breath and released his hands from where they were still clasped behind his back. There was nothing for it, nothing that he could do, and nothing more that he could say other than this. It was the only choice open to him, the only thing that would save not only Lady Hyacinth's reputation but also save her from Lord Sunderland.

"Well, Lady Venables, it seems that you have stolen my moment! I thought that we might have the opportunity to share this with Lord and Lady Coatbridge first, but alas, it seems quite impossible." With a grand smile which, he prayed, covered the fear rushing through him and the worry that was slowly beginning to consume him, Samuel turned and held out one hand to Lady Hyacinth. "Much to my great joy, Lady Hyacinth has chosen to accept my hand in marriage."

CHAPTER FOURTEEN

Hyacinth did not know what to say. When Lord Sunderland had grabbed her hand and yanked her into the library, Hyacinth had been so caught by fear she had not been able to make a single sound. What had made matters worse was that her very own mother and sister had not appeared to notice her absence for none had come after her! Thus, she had been trapped by Lord Sunderland's overbearing presence, seeing him leering at her and being overwhelmed with so much dread and fear that her legs had begun to buckle under her. How horrific the situation had been for her! When he had first pulled her in, she had managed to free herself from him, praying that some other young ladies would be in the room so that she might go to speak with them, but much to her horror, the library had been empty. Lord Sunderland had grabbed at her again, pulling her to the shadows and making all sorts of distressing remarks which had both terrified and sickened Hyacinth.

And now, yet again, Lord Thorne was coming to rescue her.

"You... you are engaged to this young lady?" Lady Venables sounded utterly astonished, though Lord Thorne quickly nodded, his hand still held out towards Hyacinth. "You came in here with her and with Lord Sunderland to propose?"

"I did, yes." Lord Thorne sounded so confident that Hyacinth knew there was nothing she could say to alter this present course. The only thing she could do was accept this new circumstance, whether she wanted it to be so or not. "We are now engaged and, if you would not mind, I must take my betrothed to go and speak to Lady Coatbridge, who, I believe, is just outside the library in the hallway."

Hyacinth grasped Lord Thorne's hand and he quickly lifted it to settle on his arm. Lady Venables let out an exclamation, followed by swiftly congratulating Lord Thorne and Hyacinth herself, though to Hyacinth, it seemed to be only a buzzing that ran through her ears. Lord Thorne lifted their joined hands for a moment as the news spread around the room, only to release it but set it quickly on his arm. Hyacinth felt as though she were in a dream, her whole body feeling both light and weak at the very same time.

"Do you wish to tell your mother or shall I?"

Hyacinth looked into Lord Thorne's eyes as they stopped by the door of the library, barely able to take in what he was asking her.

"I will have to apologize to your father for my lack of propriety, for I ought to have asked him first, I know," he continued, speaking to her as though she were able to take everything in, as though this was a perfectly normal situation. "Though I doubt there will be much complaint."

"We... " Hyacinth squeezed her eyes closed, wobbling slightly. "We are engaged? Truly?"

There was a long pause and when Hyacinth opened her eyes to look, Lord Thorne was frowning.

"Yes, we are engaged," he said, quietly, so that no one else could hear. "You must pretend that this has been expected and that you are delighted. We can talk about all that has happened and the details of it all later." Snapping his fingers at a nearby footman, he took a glass from the tray held by him and handed it to Hyacinth. "Take a sip of wine. It will help you."

Hyacinth did as she was asked, feeling as though she had no recourse other than to do what he asked her.

"I could not let you be forced into matrimony with Lord Sunderland," he continued, now leading her through the door and into the hallway. "Nor could I let you bear the disgrace that came from his actions. Thus, we are now engaged and we *shall* marry."

The decisiveness in his voice made Hyacinth go hot all over, followed by an icy chill that sent goosebumps over her skin. It was not that she felt upset over the thought of marrying Lord Thorne, it was more that she was so completely overwhelmed that she could barely catch her breath.

"I shall tell them, yes?" Lord Thorne's voice was gentler now, though the sidelong look he gave her still spoke of concern. "You are too astonished still, I think."

It was all Hyacinth could do to nod.

"Oh, there you are!" A warm smile and friendly voice made Hyacinth's shock fade just a little as Lady Eve approached. "I was just saying to your mother that – "

"Eve." Hyacinth released Lord Thorne's arm and took her friend's instead. "I must speak with you." She looked to Lord Thorne, seeing him frown at her moving away from him. "Lord Thorne, I think my father will be in the card room. You might be best placed to speak with him directly."

Lord Thorne's expression cleared. "Of course." Reaching out, he caught her fingers and pressed them lightly, his eyes fixing to hers. "I will return as quickly as I can. Pray do not speak to your mother until I am present with you."

A lump came into Hyacinth's throat at his consideration and kindness and she nodded, blinking furiously so as to keep the tears in her eyes from spilling down onto her cheeks. This, in turn, seemed to frighten Lady Eve, for her expression changed in an instant. Her eyes widened, her face lost color and she took Hyacinth's other hand in her own, leaning closer to her.

"Whatever has happened, Hyacinth? What does Lord Thorne mean about speaking to your father?" Her eyes searched Hyacinth's. "Did you speak with him? Did you ask him about the riddles?"

Closing her eyes to garner a little more composure, Hyacinth took in three long breaths and then let them out again before she had enough strength to answer. "Eve, you must keep this entirely to yourself," she began, as her friend nodded fervently. "It seems... it seems as though I am now engaged to Lord Thorne."

The words did not only bring a reaction from Lady Eve, who immediately gasped in astonishment and gripped Hyacinth's hand but Hyacinth herself, much to her shame, began to cry. Tears fell to her cheeks like rain and though Lady Eve pulled her away quickly to a quieter part of the room, a few murmurs followed after her. Soon, she knew, the news would soon be spread through the room and all and sundry would know that she was now engaged to the Marquess of Thorne.

"How did this happen?" Lady Eve asked, handing Hyacinth a handkerchief. "I am sorry to be so blunt but you must dry your eyes quickly else the *ton* will begin to whisper about your present state."

"They will, mayhap, think me overwhelmed by happiness," Hyacinth sniffed, pressing the handkerchief to her eyes. "Oh, Eve, it was quite dreadful." She shook her head and looked down at the floor, still feeling a trembling in her frame. "Lord Sunderland grabbed at me before I could even realize what was happening and he pulled me into the library. There was no one else present and his intentions quickly became clear!"

"Did your mother not notice? Your father?"

Hyacinth shook her head, the ache in her throat growing steadily. "My father had already gone to the card room and my mother and sister did not appear to see that I was gone from their company. I thought that my mother might follow after me, fearful as to what Lord Sunderland was to do but... but she did not." Closing her eyes and fighting another wave of tears, Hyacinth took in a shuddering breath. "It shows you how little I mean to them, how much of a shadow I am."

Lady Eve pressed Hyacinth's hand. "That is their mistake."

Hyacinth nodded, trying to force herself to believe it. "I was saved by Lord Thorne. I do not know why he came into the room nor what it was he intended but he came to pull Lord Sunderland away. However, when other guests came into the room, it became clear that I was not to escape."

"Oh, my dear friend." Lady Eve's voice was soft. "You thought your reputation was at an end."

"Worse than that," Hyacinth whispered, no longer able

to put any strength into her voice, "I thought that I would have to wed Lord Sunderland."

Lady Eve's face went very red indeed, evidently angry over what it was Lord Sunderland had done. She did not speak for some moments, turning her head away, her lips pinched. Hyacinth said nothing, fighting with her own emotions, aware that, at any moment, Lord Thorne would return and the news would soon be told to everyone present.

"Lord Thorne stepped in and took his place," Lady Eve said, after a good few minutes. "He said he would marry you?"

Nodding, Hyacinth let out a slow breath, relieved that the tears in her eyes had now been pushed back. "He said to Lady Venables, the lady who demanded to know what was happening, that he had come into the library with me to propose and that I had accepted him. And now, there is nothing for me to do but marry him!"

"That is not so bad, is it?" Lady Eve murmured, glancing around the room as if she feared being overheard. "He is a Marquess of good standing and with an excellent fortune. Yes, I am aware of the difficulties that the riddles presents but all the same, this could be an excellent match."

Hyacinth could not answer, still struggling to comprehend it all.

"You are overcome with shock though, of course." Lady Eve smiled briefly. "Forgive me, I should have seen that."

"I will have to present a joyous expression to my mother, sister, and the rest of the other guests," Hyacinth murmured, turning her head just in time to see not only Lord Thorne but her father coming to join her. "I will have to pretend that I think it all a truly delightful thing."

"And you can do it." With another press of her hand,

Lady Eve took a small step back. "Make them believe that you are overcome with joy and consider the truth of it all later. Think on what is important now, not on what must be done."

Hyacinth nodded, appreciating her friend's advice but nothing more could be said given that her father was only a step or two away.

"Hyacinth!" he exclaimed, a broad smile on his usual serious face. "What wonderful news! Come now, let us go and find your mother."

This was more effusive than her father had ever really been and Hyacinth, a little surprised, tried to force a smile. "Of course, Father." She accepted Lord Thorne's arm and, with a glance towards Lady Eve, permitted him to lead her away. Her father had always been rather silent and certainly very absent during her time in London, preferring to give the responsibility for her future to Lady Coatbridge. Now, it seemed, he was to be very present indeed, as though he had been the one behind the engagement.

"My dear, there you are." Lord Coatbridge beamed at his wife, though Lady Coatbridge did not smile, her gaze darting from Hyacinth to Lord Thorne and back again. "I have just heard the news from Lord Thorne, though half the house is abuzz with it now!"

"News?" It was Rose who spoke rather than Lady Coatbridge, her eyebrows pulling into a frown. "What news?"

"About your sister's engagement!" Lord Coatbridge exclaimed, bringing both a gasp of shock from Lady Rose and an exclamation of seeming delight from Lady Coatbridge. "Lord Thorne has asked for her hand and not only does he have my blessing, Hyacinth has accepted him – and has done so this very evening! Is that not wonderful?"

For what was the second time that evening, Hyacinth

found herself overwhelmed completely. It was not only her mother that came to congratulate her and ask her how such a thing had come to be, but so many of the other guests also decided to join in, overhearing the news from Lord Coatbridge given that he had spoken in a very loud voice indeed, which was most unusual. Hyacinth was dazed, having her hand shaken by one person only for another to embrace her. Lord Thorne was beaming, seeming to be both proud and pleased at the reaction to their engagement, as if all of it was quite real and fully expected and as if he truly felt glad to be marrying her.

"How did you manage this?"

A tight hand grabbed at Hyacinth's arm, pulling her closer and Hyacinth started in surprise, turning her attention to Rose.

"You know very well that *I* am to marry first," Rose hissed, nothing but venom in her expression. "*I* am the one who has the beauty, the elegance and the refinement. You are nothing but a wallflower! What did you do to make a Marquess seek to marry you?"

Yet another shock rippled over Hyacinth as she looked into her sister's eyes, seeing the anger there. Did Rose truly believe that Hyacinth had done something improper to have Lord Thorne ask for her hand? She blinked, then shook her head, glancing around her as she became a little afraid that someone else would overhear Rose speak so. "I have done nothing, Rose. Do not think that I have behaved in any way improperly."

"Oh, but I *do* think so." Anger pulling her lips flat, her eyes flashing, Rose leaned closer to Hyacinth as though it was only the two of them in the room. "Whatever you did, I will expose it. I will – "

"Do excuse me."

Before Hyacinth could respond, none other than Lord Thorne came to stand beside her, though his gaze was fixed on Rose who immediately went a shade of scarlet.

"You are congratulating your sister, no doubt?" Lord Thorne took Hyacinth's hand in his own, pressing it lightly. "You must be very happy for her, I am sure."

Rose began to stammer but Lord Thorne continued on, speaking over her though Hyacinth could not tell whether or not he had heard anything Rose had said.

"I do hope that you are as contented with our engagement as I am, Lady Hyacinth," he said, making a slow-growing heat begin to flood through Hyacinth as she looked into his eyes, seeing him now turning his full attention towards her. "I understand that I surprised you with it but I could not help it."

"I see now that you could not." Hyacinth offered him a small smile, knowing that there was a good deal more for them to say to each other though they could not do so at this present moment. He had come to her aid and had ended up an engaged gentleman and though relief was one of the emotions she felt, Hyacinth could not help but feel a trifle guilty, though she knew none of this was her own doing. Something within her desperately wanted him to have even the smallest amount of happiness at their connection, wanted him to feel even a little joy at their engagement but she could not be sure of it.

As though he had been able to read her thoughts, Lord Thorne moved a fraction closer to her, his eyes fixed on hers and making her feel as though she were the only one standing there. "I am glad that you are to be my wife, Hyacinth."

At this, Hyacinth felt her whole being slowly begin to melt into a puddle of relief. She could not look anywhere else but into his face as he smiled, a gentle look in his eyes that she had never seen before.

"How wonderful." Rose's tone was heavy, making it clear that she did not truly feel any of the words she spoke. "Of course, I am quite delighted at my sister's engagement, as you have said, Lord Thorne. I am sure you could not have found anyone better suited."

Lord Thorne's smile only grew but he did not so much as glance towards Rose, still gazing into Hyacinth's eyes. "Indeed, I think that is quite true," he said, softly. "No one better indeed."

CHAPTER FIFTEEN

I must tell her the truth.

Samuel turned expectantly as the door to his study opened and the butler came in. He was waiting for Lady Hyacinth to come to call, along with either her mother or father and quite how he was to tell her the truth about the riddles when they were present also, he did not know – but it had to be done.

Instead, Lord Elledge came into the room.

"Good gracious, I hear that you are engaged!" he said, striding across the room to shake Samuel's hand. "However did that come about?"

Samuel offered his friend a wry smile. "It was a little unexpected."

"I should say so!"

With a sigh, Samuel gestured for his friend to sit down. "Lord Sunderland did not behave well and again, I had to come to the rescue of another young lady."

"And you ended up proposing to her?" Lord Elledge asked, sounding incredulous though, at a look from Samuel, he caught his breath, his eyes widening. "You took the place of Lord Sunderland so she would not have to marry him?"

Samuel winced. "You make it sound as though I was forced to do so."

Lord Elledge looked back at him in question but Samuel only shook his head.

"I had a choice," he explained. "I could have permitted Lord Sunderland to take the lady and do right by her, or I could have permitted him to step back from it all and leave her to the *ton*'s whispers."

A few lines formed on Lord Elledge's brow. "But then her reputation would have been quite ruined."

"Indeed it would have been."

His friend clicked his tongue and scowled. "Lord Sunderland ought to have done what he ought."

Again, Samuel winced. "But could you imagine what Lady Hyacinth's life would have been like, had she married him?"

This made Lord Elledge's expression darken all the more. "That is not something I had given an immediate thought to."

"I did." Recalling just how upset Lady Hyacinth had been when he had first found her, Samuel's heart twisted in his chest. "She was quite broken, Elledge. Lord Sunderland had yanked her into that room without rhyme nor reason and, much to her horror, it had been quite empty so there was no one else to turn to. Her mother did not see that she was absent and thus, Lord Sunderland was able to cause her a great deal of distress."

"How awful."

"I can no longer be associated with him," Samuel continued, darkly. "I do not want to be his company any longer and, to be quite honest, I think it would be wise for us to perhaps whisper here and there about his true character."

Lord Elledge nodded firmly. "To protect other young ladies."

"Indeed."

His friend smiled darkly. "He will not thank us for it but I do not care for that. Not after he has behaved so dreadfully. Though," he continued, tipping his head to one side as his eyes fixed on Samuel, "you must tell me whether or not you truly do care for Lady Hyacinth. I know that you have been battling your feelings when it comes to the lady but I am also *keenly* aware of just how little you wanted marriage."

"That has all changed now." Samuel offered his friend a slightly rueful smile. "The truth is, I was hoping to speak with Lady Hyacinth at the soiree last evening. I had given in to all that I felt and wanted very much to tell her the truth, even if it was to be expressed in a somewhat clumsy manner." A sudden weight dropped into his stomach. "I wanted also to tell her about the riddles, before I told the others in the *ton*."

This made Lord Elledge's eyebrows shoot up.

"I recognize what a fool I have been and how much I have considered my pride more than anything else," Samuel said, heavily. "I ought never to have said such a foolish thing and I wanted to tell Lady Hyacinth the truth. I could not express my heart to her when there was such a thing between us."

It took a few moments for Lord Elledge to answer but when he did, it was with a broad smile. "I must say, I am glad to hear it! And a little impressed too, I confess. I did not think that there would ever be a time when you set your pride away, aside from yourself. But now it seems that you have done so."

"Only because of what I feel for her," Samuel admitted. "But now I must find a way to tell her everything"

Lord Elledge shrugged "Then do so."

"I cannot." Samuel's lips pulled a downwards. "Her mother is to come to call this afternoon and I will not be able to speak with Lady Hyacinth alone. In fact, I do not know when I will be able to do so!"

Lord Elledge chuckled. "There is a simple answer!"

"Oh?"

"Tell her."

Samuel frowned. "What do you mean?"

"Tell Lady Hyacinth that you wish to speak with her alone and tell her mother also." Lord Elledge shrugged. "Walk in the park if you wish but it is almost expected for an engaged couple to be alone in each other's company for a few minutes here and there." He chuckled again as Samuel's frown lifted. "You are not a single gentleman any longer, my friend. You can be alone with your betrothed for a short while at least, without anyone lifting an eyebrow."

Musing, Samuel slowly began to nod, recognizing now that his change in status did mean a little more freedom... and with it, came a small frisson of excitement. Or was it worry?

"She cannot step back from our engagement now," he murmured aloud, as Lord Elledge nodded. "All the same, I confess that I am a little afraid as to what she will say when I tell her the truth. I do not want to have a wife who is ashamed of me." His shoulders dropped. "Though I am still very much ashamed of myself."

Lord Elledge smiled encouragingly. "You have already shown her that you have great kindness and consideration in your heart," he said, as Samuel swallowed hard, trying not to let his worry grasp hold of him. "Trust her with the truth and pray that all will be well."

"It is very good to see you again." Samuel smiled as warmly as he could to Lady Hyacinth, though she was not able to hold his gaze for long, it seemed, given how quickly she turned her face away, looking to her mother instead. "I do hope that all is well?"

Lady Coatbridge settled her hands in her lap and sighed contentedly, a bright smile on her face. "How could it not be, Lord Thorne? You have agreed to marry my daughter and now a wedding must be planned!"

"Indeed it must." Samuel glanced from Lady Coatbridge to Lady Rose to Lady Hyacinth. "There is much to be done and I am very much looking forward to our wedding day, Lady Hyacinth."

For the first time since she had stepped into the room, Lady Hyacinth smiled, a flush of color rising into her cheeks. "As am I, Lord Thorne."

"Might I ask, Lord Thorne, precisely what happened last evening?" Lady Coatbridge spoke again, a lightness in her voice that Samuel thought to be a little false. "It all came as a great surprise to me, for though I had seen you often in Hyacinth's company, you had not come to call or to take tea or the like."

Samuel glanced at Lady Hyacinth and saw her shoulders drop just a little. The next glance told him that Lady Rose had a small, supercilious smile on her face which made his own heart sink.

What was it that Lady Rose had said to her mother? He had seen her speak ill of Lady Hyacinth before – and publicly too. Had she suggested something improper to her mother as regards this engagement? Would she dare whisper rumors through the *beau monde* solely because of her jealousy or resentment?

Hearing a scratch at the door, Samuel waited until the tea tray was brought in and set down before he continued, relieved to have the next few minutes to gather his thoughts. Once the maid had gone, he looked directly back into Lady Coatbridge's face. "That is quite true, Lady Coatbridge. I did not come to call, I did not ask to take tea and the like and I certainly did not ask to court Lady Hyacinth!"

"Then why did you propose so suddenly?" Lady Coatbridge asked, with a boldness that surprised Samuel a little. "I do not understand."

Lady Rose broke into the conversation, her face glowing with a light that Samuel could not understand. "Might I pour the tea, Lord Thorne?"

He nodded but barely gave her a look, his whole being desiring now to be close to Lady Hyacinth, to pull her out of this trouble that, to his mind, her sister had placed upon her. "It was a surprise, I know. Even Lady Hyacinth was a little astonished at it all, were you not?" Pinning a smile to his face, he looked to Lady Hyacinth and saw her nod, though her face was a little paler now. "I even astonished myself, Lady Coatbridge, but that is because I have spent many a year determining that marriage is not something I desired."

"And yet, out of every young lady in London, you chose to engage yourself to my sister?" It was Lady Rose's turn to speak boldly now, it seemed, and she did not so much as flush hot when Samuel sent a sharp eye in her direction. "It has been said before – and I am sure you are aware of it – that Hyacinth is a wallflower! I told you that her dance card had never been filled before and yet, you proposed to *her*?" She tossed her head. "It is all a little unusual."

Samuel's stomach turned over on itself as Lady Hyacinth dropped her head. He had no true knowledge as to what Lady Rose might have said, both to her mother and to Lady Hyacinth, but he could imagine what her words had done. No doubt she had complained to her mother that *she* was not the one engaged first, that Hyacinth must have done something to force Samuel's hand... and Samuel was not about to permit her to cling to that notion nor to her injured pride.

"Falling in love is a little unusual."

The words came out of his mouth with such a certainty that Samuel had to pause to give himself a moment to consider what he both said and felt. Was that what he truly had for Lady Hyacinth, held tightly in his heart? To be falling in love with her was not only significant, it was overwhelming but, at the very same time, Samuel recognized just how much joy now exploded through him as he confessed it aloud.

"Love?" Lady Coatbridge's eyes widened, shooting a look to Lady Rose that confirmed to Samuel that they had been speaking poorly of Lady Hyacinth and her sudden engagement. "You surely do not mean to say that you have such a deep affection for my daughter?"

Samuel drew himself up. "That is precisely what I mean to say, Lady Coatbridge."

"But – but you did not take tea!" Lady Rose exclaimed, sounding quite horrified as if he had just said something truly despicable. "You did not come to call nor to ask to court her, so how can you have had such feelings?"

Turning his full attention towards Lady Hyacinth, Samuel waited for her to raise her eyes to his. When she finally did so, there was a flush of color in her cheeks but a brightness in her eyes which spoke of surprise but also of happiness.

"Yes, I did not do any of those things. I will admit to you all that, at the start of the Season, I rejected all thought of matrimony, telling not only myself but my friends that I did not want to marry until I had no other choice but to do so. When the pressing responsibility of producing an heir became too great, I would select a young lady, marry her, and have that responsibility taken care of. However," he continued, seeing Lady Rose attempting to speak again, "that all changed the moment I set eyes upon Lady Hyacinth."

"Goodness." Lady Coatbridge sounded completely astonished, her eyes still round with surprise. "Can that truly be so?"

"Why would it not be?" Samuel asked, his own heart erupting at the smile that began to spread across Lady Hyacinth's face. "To my mind, there is no one more beautiful, more delightful, and more elegant than Hyacinth and in recognizing that, I gave up fighting against my past desires and begged her to be my wife." All of this, Samuel recognized, was the truth, save for the latter few words. She might be considered a wallflower, might be considered to lack beauty in comparison to her sister but Samuel saw none of that. Lady Hyacinth was more to him than any other young lady. It was because of her and her alone that he had put his determination to forget about matrimony for as long as he could to one side.

"Well, I certainly did not expect you to say such a thing as that!" Lady Coatbridge exclaimed, speaking, again, with that frankness that Samuel found rather surprising. "I always expected that Hyacinth would marry her second cousin, for we did not think that she would do very well."

Samuel shook his head, making Lady Coatbridge's face flush with what he hoped was embarrassment. "It is not about whether *she* has done well, Lady Coatbridge, but rather how well *I* have done in securing her hand. There are many in the *ton* who might overlook a wallflower but I shall always be grateful for the moment I was introduced to her. It has altered everything about me and about my life. I cannot wait for the day I shall stand up in church and make my vows. The day that Lady Hyacinth becomes my wife shall be the happiest of all my days, I am quite sure."

The room was silent for some moments as all three ladies looked back at him. Lady Rose had gone a shade of puce, Lady Coatbridge was still red with embarrassment but it was Lady Hyacinth that caught Samuel's full attention. Her smile was tender, a gentle sweetness in her expression that he wanted to cling to. It took him all of his strength not to make his way across the room to sit beside her, wanting to feel her hand in his, to have her closer to him than ever before.

"Might we take a walk tomorrow afternoon, Lady Hyacinth?" he asked, abruptly changing the subject. "I thought, mayhap, St James' Park? We could walk together and speak without interruption, if you should like it?"

The light in her eyes only grew as she nodded, her smile growing all the more.

"Excellent," Samuel replied, hope blossoming in his heart. Perhaps, even with all his mistakes and foolishness, he might find a happiness still – a happiness that, he knew, he did not truly deserve.

CHAPTER SIXTEEN

"Good afternoon, Lord Thorne." Hyacinth took his arm practically the very moment he came close enough for her to do so, relieved to be away from her mother and sister who, Lady Coatbridge had promised, would be a short distance behind them.

"It brings my heart great joy to see you," came the reply, his eyes fixed on hers. "Goodness, Hyacinth, you cannot know how much I have longed to be alone in your company!"

Hyacinth did not respond with anything other than a smile. It was exactly the very same feeling she had experienced, for now that the shock and the surprise at her engagement had faded, it had left her with entirely different emotions. Emotions that spoke of relief and happiness and even joy – and after their conversation the previous afternoon, those feelings had only grown. The only shadow over it all was Hyacinth's worry that he had not spoken the truth of his heart, that those words had been said only to break apart any concern that her mother or Rose had about the engagement, and he had done so very well indeed.

"Might I ask you something?" Lord Thorne asked, as they began to walk, arm in arm, through the park. "Did your sister have anything to say about our engagement?"

Hyacinth bit her lip, then nodded slowly. "You recognized that from our visit yesterday."

"I did."

"She has been jealous," Hyacinth admitted, letting out a sigh. "It has been painful to hear though your words to me yesterday did seem to bring some relief to that. She no longer has my mother's ear."

Lord Thorne's lips lifted. "I am glad to hear it."

That did not bring Hyacinth the reassurance she wanted. She wanted to hear him say that everything he had said had been the truth, that he had, in fact, fallen in love with her and was truly eager to marry her... but he did not. Instead, a frown swept across his forehead, his expression now heavy and Hyacinth's heart slowly began to sink.

"There is something that I must say to you, Hyacinth." Lord Thorne glanced at her but then turned his gaze away again, a redness coming into his cheeks. "I have every intention of doing what I must as regards this matter but you must know of it first."

A thrill raced up Hyacinth's spine as she saw the heat in his face, wondering what it was that he wanted to say. Could it be the confession she was hoping for? Would he tell her that he did have an affection for her after all?

"Let me tell you now before I lose my courage." Lord Thorne offered her a slightly rueful smile but there was fear in his eyes that was unmistakable, making Hyacinth's heart lurch. "I do not know what you will think of me after this and, truth be told, I did have an intention to speak to you of this before Lord Sunderland behaved as he did. I do not want you to think that I am only telling you this now because we are engaged."

Understanding slowly began to grow in Hyacinth's mind, her eyebrows lifting gently. Was this about the riddles? Was that what he had wanted to tell her before Lord Sunderland had snatched her as he did?

"I understand if you think me foolish, if you think me ridiculous, and if you think me despicable," Lord Thorne continued, his voice sounding heavy. "I look at my actions and I find myself mortified over my lack of sense and, truth be told, the pride which so clearly fills me."

"Lord Thorne," Hyacinth began, speaking slowly as her own heart began to quicken, aware that she would have to soon tell him the truth. "Are you speaking about the riddles in The London Chronicle?"

This made him turn sharply, her hand falling to her side as he stepped back just a little, staring into her eyes. Hyacinth pressed her lips tightly together, not certain whether she ought to say more and finding herself a little afraid that he was about to be very angry indeed with her.

Instead, Lord Thorne let out a snort of rueful laughter, shaking his head as he rubbed one hand over his eyes. "There was always something in me that said you were suspicious of me. From the very beginning, I thought that you were not sure I was telling the truth."

"And you were not." Hyacinth let this come out as a statement rather than a question, her heart pounding furiously as she looked into the eyes of the gentleman she was to marry, praying that he would not be angry with her because of this. "I knew you were not."

Lord Thorne closed his eyes, his lips still quirked just a little. "Indeed, I was not."

"But you told the *ton* that you were."

He nodded, looking back at her steadily now. "Yes, I did."

"Why?" Hyacinth, already aware of the answer, chose to let him speak in his own words, letting him find the right way to explain himself. She waited and watched, seeing him look away, dropping his head and then blowing out a long breath.

"Because, my dear Hyacinth, I am a gentleman who has fought with arrogance and pride," came the answer, his shoulders dropping. "That is why. I have always found myself rather prideful though I have never done anything about the matter, believing myself to be just as a gentleman ought. I have told myself over and over again that every gentleman is arrogant, that it is unusual for a gentleman *not* to be so! But even if that were the case, not every gentleman is the sort who would lie about something like the riddles, would they?"

Hyacinth swallowed at the tightness in her throat. "Might I ask why you chose to lie about being the writer of the riddles? Yes, I understand that you might have been fighting with arrogance but why specifically did you state that you wrote them when you did not?"

Lord Thorne closed his eyes. "I did so out of mortification, truth be told. It is linked to my pride, I know, for I did not want it to be injured. You may have already understood but I did not know the answer to the riddles and I was too ashamed to admit it." Opening his eyes again, he winced visibly as he returned his gaze to her. "Thus, out of my mouth came the most ridiculous, foolish lie where I pretended that I had written the riddles and *that* was the reason that I did not know the answers. It was so that I did not spoil them for those who were seeking the answers."

Hyacinth waited for a crash of anger or flare of upset to

burst through her chest but to her surprise, nothing came. Instead, all there was within her was a gentle trickle of relief which, slowly but surely, grew into a torrent. A smile began to spread across her face, though Hyacinth quickly pushed it away, knowing that there was yet more for her to say, more for her to reveal.

"I do not think that you are angry with me." Lord Thorne sounded surprised, the corners of his eyes rounding. "That is astonishing for I am certainly deserving of your frustration and upset."

"That may be so," Hyacinth agreed, choosing not to deny it, "but I confess to be glad that you have told me the truth, Lord Thorne. And to know that you desired to do so long before our unexpected engagement means a great deal to me."

A hint of a smile brushed across his lips though his eyes still searched hers.

"You are right that I suspected you were not telling me the truth when it came to those riddles," she continued, feeling as if someone were grasping tight at her throat and squeezing it such was the tension beginning to flood her. "I confess that I did see you upset over being unable to answer the riddles but never did I expect for you to state that it was because *you* were the author of them!"

Lord Thorne's color began to rise again. "It was a moment of foolishness that I now deeply regret," he said, quietly. "The author of the riddles was very upset that I had claimed his work for my own, for the answers to the riddles were all directed towards me." He smiled tightly. "Though I did write two of my own and send them into The London Chronicle."

Hyacinth nodded, speaking without thinking. "I saw

them. They were an attempt to express your sorrow over what you had done, yes?"

Something flashed in his eyes. "Yes, that is quite so." The edge of his mouth lifted just a little. "You are quite a marvel, Lady Hyacinth. You were able to discern that I was the one who had sent those two riddles into the paper? You could tell that their answers were so different, mayhap that they must have come from me?"

Licking her lips, Hyacinth let out a slow breath as she fought to find the right words to tell him the truth. He had been honest with her, she recognized, and she wanted very much to be so with him so that this entire matter could be set aside, but it was difficult for her to do so. Everything she wanted to say was jumbling in her mind, her thoughts tumbling this way and that, combined with the fear of what he might say or do once she had told him the truth.

"Hyacinth?" Lord Thorne moved a fraction closer, his eyes holding a concern now as his hand found hers. "What is the matter?"

Setting her shoulders back, Hyacinth looked up at him and chose to speak the simple truth. "I did not suspect, Lord Thorne. I knew without doubt that you were not writing the riddles."

Not looking anywhere other than his face, Hyacinth said nothing more but waited for understanding to come into his eyes. It took some moments, for he both blinked and then frowned, only for then his eyes to flare wide as he hauled in a breath.

When his mouth fell open, she could only nod.

"You... you mean to say that *you*... " It seemed he could not finish his sentence for the words ended abruptly as he turned away from her for only a moment, rubbing one hand down his face before swinging back towards her. Hyacinth could barely breathe, twisting her fingers together in front of her as she waited for his response.

And then, Lord Thorne began to laugh. He laughed so hard that tears came into his eyes and Hyacinth, relief swamping her, closed her eyes and smiled. It was all going to be quite all right, she realized. He was not going to be angry with her, was not going to be upset with all that she had done. Nor was he going to berate her, question her, mock her or even doubt her. The truth had been expressed and he had accepted it without too much concern, it seemed, given the laughter that poured from him.

"Is... is everything quite all right?"

Hyacinth glanced over her shoulder as her mother and sister came closer, mayhap a little concerned about Lord Thorne's present state and the attention he was drawing from others. "Yes, Mama," she answered, as Lord Thorne, still grinning, reached out to take her hand. "Everything is quite wonderful."

CHAPTER SEVENTEEN

"You mean to say that *she* – "

Samuel nodded, a broad smile on his face as Lord Elledge stared at him in clear astonishment. "Yes. That is precisely what I mean."

His friend's eyes squeezed closed and he gave himself a small shake as though he could not quite make sense of what he had heard, as if the music from the orchestra had confused what he had heard. Samuel said nothing more, waiting for Lord Elledge to take in what had been said, just as he had done a sennight ago. The shock of hearing that Lady Hyacinth had been the one writing the riddles – though she had let him understand that for himself – had been so great, it had practically shattered him, such was his surprise. He did not know what to do or what to say, staring at his betrothed as his heart had melted within him.

And then, laughter had come. He felt himself so utterly foolish at that moment, realizing that he had been playing a pretense with someone who already knew the truth and that it had been *she*, in fact, who had been playing with him! She had been the one who had written the riddles with their answers pointing directly towards him. She had been the one who had used her great skill to let him know that she was aware of his lies. She had been the one who had shown such mercy, for she had not told the *ton* the truth even though she could easily have done so. Samuel had seen her in a new light at that moment, aware now of just how much he had been blessed with in her... and feeling just how little he deserved it.

"I can hardly believe it!" Lord Elledge shook his head, then pulled out his handkerchief and mopped at his forehead. "She and I did have a conversation at one point, where we were both aware that neither of us trusted your word in all of this, but never did I think that she would have been the one writing the riddles for The London Chronicle!"

"I was as astonished as you," Samuel admitted, smiling. "But I do not think that I can express just how much relief I felt in hearing the truth of it all. Indeed, I was so overwhelmed by my own sense of foolishness, that I could not help but laugh!"

"Laugh?" Lord Elledge blinked then chuckled. "Goodness, I do wish I had been there to witness it! I do not think I have ever heard you laugh at your own foolishness before."

Smiling ruefully, Samuel spread out his hands. "That is quite true, I am sure. But now, because of her I can see just how ridiculous I have been and how much now needs to change. And I have every intention of altering myself entirely, to rid myself of all pride and deceit. Now that I have her, now that she is to be my wife, I want to be only the very best of gentlemen for her." A stab of pain made him grimace. "I am well aware of my failings and how much I have fallen short thus far, but Lady Hyacinth is nothing but forgiveness and kindness."

Lord Elledge smiled. "It seems to me as though your feelings for the lady have grown significantly since we last spoke."

Considering this, Samuel nodded, finding a great peace in accepting all that he felt. "Yes, I would agree with that. My heart is full of her for now that I see her as she truly is, with all her intelligence and beauty, I feel nothing but gratitude for her and for her acceptance of me."

Putting one hand on Samuel's shoulder, Lord Elledge beamed at him. "It seems that all you once rejected, you are now delighting in! I am very glad for you, my friend."

"I thank you. Though," Samuel continued, looking around the room, "tonight, I must make everything right."

This made Lord Elledge frown, his hand dropping away. "What do you mean?"

"I mean that I must tell the *beau monde* that it is not I who writes for The London Chronicle but it is Hyacinth herself." Seeing Lord Elledge's frown lift, Samuel shrugged. "It is not going to be a pleasant experience, I know, but I must do it. For her sake, at the very least. I want the *ton* and even her own family to see just how much of a treasure she is."

"Then I wish you very well," came the reply. "I presume the lady knows about this?"

"Knows about what?"

Lady Hyacinth's voice cut through their conversation and Samuel twisted around to see her standing a little behind him, a light smile on her face. "Hyacinth." He smiled and took her hand, lifting it to his lips and, as he kissed the back of her hand, feeling a rush of desire tearing through him. "I was just speaking with Lord Elledge."

"Good evening, Lord Elledge," she answered, her

brown eyes going between him and Samuel. "I do hope there is nothing you are hiding from me, Thorne?"

Samuel chuckled and squeezed her hand. "You are suspicious of me, my dear. Well, I shall not keep it from you." Pushing away the nervousness that began to wrap around him, Samuel took in a steadying breath and then, with a smile to Hyacinth, stepped out into the center of the ballroom. Someone tapped a glass lightly, alerting the guests to his presence and it did not take more than a few moments before every eye in the ballroom was upon him.

The smile on Samuel's face faltered. There were a good many guests present and to open his mouth and admit to all of his foolishness was a little frightening. He did not know what reaction he would receive from the *ton*, quite sure that some of them would mock him, some would laugh and some begin to whisper to their acquaintances. Whispers and rumors might fly all through London... but he could not help that, he reasoned. He was the one who had made this mess in the beginning by his own foolishness and it was about time that he set it right.

"Thank you all for your attention." With a bow, Samuel lifted his gaze to the crowd, letting it sweep across each and every face. "As you know, Lady Hyacinth and I are now betrothed and the wedding shall take place in a month from now."

This was met by applause and Samuel could not help but smile, despite his nervousness.

"I cannot tell you how overjoyed I was when Lady Hyacinth accepted my proposal," he said, knowing full well that while he had never truly proposed to the lady, his joy had been great once he had realized what happiness his future now held. "I think that she is the most remarkable creature in all of England, though I am also sure that every gentleman thinks such a thing of his betrothed!" A few murmurs and smiles met this remark, though Samuel finally pulled his gaze towards Lady Hyacinth, knowing that she did not know what it was he intended to say. He had to hope that she would be glad of it, for they had never spoken of what ought to be done as regarded the truth about the riddles.

"I have thrown this ball in her honor," he continued, swallowing hard as he fought for the right words to say. "Because she has given me more than I ever expected, even more than I knew. Not only is she kind, beautiful, generous, and considerate, she is also forgiving and that is what has brought us closer together."

Lady Hyacinth's smile began to fade though she did not shake her head at him nor whisper to him not to say a word. She was waiting, he realized, to know what it was he wanted to express and, with another small nod in her direction, Samuel continued, his heart pounding furiously in his chest.

"I wanted to tell you all that I have lied to you." That brought an end to the smiles on everyone's faces but Samuel continued on, refusing to be held back. "I am ashamed of myself but I must also be honest, for I have injured the person I love the most and it is to her that this apology is made." Throwing out one hand towards Hyacinth, he waited for a moment, seeing the eyes of every guest turning towards her. "Ladies and gentlemen, I told you that I was the one who wrote the riddles in The London Chronicle. I told you that I was the one who put my time and energy into creating such incredible twisting secrets for you all to decipher...but I was not." Hearing a few gasps, he lifted his shoulders and spoke with decisiveness. "The reason I told you all such a thing is because I was not able to find the answers to the first few riddles. Rather than admitting that, I chose to lie to protect my pride. That was wrong. It took something that was not mine and took the glory away from the *true* author... Lady Hyacinth."

The room fell into complete silence for a few moments. Lady Hyacinth blushed furiously, her eyes melding to his as though she could not bring herself to look anywhere else.

And then, someone began to clap.

Samuel beamed in delight as the entire room filled with applause, his heart swelling with pride as he beckoned Lady Hyacinth to him. She glanced here and there, perhaps looking for her mother and sister – both of whom, Samuel noted, were standing with looks of complete shock on their faces – before coming out towards him. Catching her hand, Samuel bent over it and kissed it lightly before smiling into her eyes, the room reverberating with the sound of appreciation.

"I am overwhelmed," she whispered, as Samuel smiled down into her eyes. "I did not think that you would do this."

"I had no choice but to do so," he said, as she took his arm so they might walk away from the center of the room together. "I wanted to make things right and this was the only way to do it." A sudden, fierce desire gripped him, and nodding and smiling at a few of the guests who wished to speak with either himself or Lady Hyacinth, Samuel made his way directly towards the French doors, praying that she would not protest at coming with him into the gardens. The fresh air felt cool on his skin and he drew in a deep breath, a sense of freedom filing him, as if bonds he had tied about himself had finally been broken.

"You certainly did make things right," Lady Hyacinth murmured, leaning into him a little more as they walked together. "I was so very afraid of telling you the truth, fearing that you would be upset with me – angry, mayhap."

Samuel turned to face her. "I would never be angry with you," he answered, gently. "The reason I laughed was because I saw how foolish I had been and my pride, in that moment, shattered completely." Smiling, his heart quickening, he raised his hand to her cheek. "There was more that I wanted to tell you, Hyacinth, though we did not have opportunity."

Her eyes lifted to his. "Oh?"

This felt more difficult to say than the truth about the riddles! Feeling the words sticking in his throat, Samuel cleared it gently, then set his shoulders. "Hyacinth, ever since we first met, I have felt a growing connection between us. The truth is, I have felt my heart soften towards you and, as Lord Elledge knows all too well, I did not like it."

Her eyes rounded. "No?"

He shook his head. "I did not want to be drawn to you, Hyacinth. I did not want to have any feelings for you and I was determined to free myself of them."

Her shoulders dropped. "Oh."

"But I could not."

This brought her head back up in a moment, a smile beginning to press at her lips, a light sparkle in her eyes.

"The more I fought it, the more my emotions clung to you," he told her, letting his hand go to her shoulder, then to her waist. "I truly am glad to be engaged, Hyacinth, because it means now that I shall never have to let you go. My heart can continue to hold on to you, and my love for you continues to grow steadily. It confused me utterly, I will confess, but the moment I realized what it was that I felt, it was as though the entire world tipped me upside down and then set me on my feet again."

Lady Hyacinth snatched in a breath, one hand going to her mouth, her eyes flaring. Samuel, a little uncertain, made to speak, only for her to drop her hand and, much to his astonishment, fling both of her hands about his neck and lift herself up on her tiptoes to kiss him.

The second his lips touched hers, fire shot through him and burned right into his very bones. Samuel wrapped his arms about her, holding her as close as he dared as a great sway of emotion held him tightly. It was as if all that he had felt redoubled itself, pouring through him until he was filled to the very top with love.

"Oh, Thorne." Her eyes still closed, Lady Hyacinth whispered against his lips, her fingers now brushing through his hair. "We have been fighting the same battle, you and I."

This made Samuel start and Lady Hyacinth's eyes opened. "You mean - ?"

She laughed softly as she nodded. "Indeed. I drew close to you to try and force you to reveal the truth about the riddles but, in the process, I completely lost my heart." Leaning into him again, her eyes fluttered closed as the desire to kiss her again tore through Samuel. "You see, I am quite in love with you too, Lord Thorne."

EPILOGUE

Walking down the aisle of the church, Hyacinth did nothing other than fix her eyes on Lord Thorne, trying to ignore everyone else present in the church. The last four weeks had been a mixture of happiness and frustration, for though she was utterly delighted with Lord Thorne, the whispers about what he had revealed at their engagement ball had been particularly difficult to ignore. However, at the very same time, she had been overwhelmed with his determination to exalt her and her work, setting her into the *ton*'s consideration while he stepped back.

Looking forward, she caught Lord Thorne's eyes as he turned to look at her, seeing the soft smile on his lips and feeling a thrill of anticipation race through her. There had been only a few stolen moments with Lord Thorne, when she had been able to be held in his arms, when he had brought his lips gently to hers. His profession of love had filled her completely and there was nothing more that she either wanted or needed, nothing other than him.

Standing close to him made her desire for his nearness

bloom. Wishing she could take his arm, Hyacinth prayed silently for patience as the clergyman began the marriage ceremony. Opening the book of Common Prayer, the clergyman looked first to Lord Thorne and then to Hyacinth, though he smiled gently as he did so as though he truly was delighted at their connection.

"Dearly beloved, we are gathered together here in the sight of God, and in the face of this congregation to join together this Man and this Woman in holy Matrimony, which is an honorable estate, instituted of God in the time of man's innocence, signifying unto us the mystical union that is between Christ and his Church. It is not to be taken on unadvisedly, lightly, or wantonly, to satisfy men's carnal lusts but reverently, discreetly, advisedly, soberly, and in the fear of God; duly considering the causes for which Matrimony was ordained."

Hyacinth forced herself to breathe slowly, to listen to each word so that it would not simply wash over her.

"First," the clergyman continued, "marriage was ordained for the procreation of children, to be brought up in the fear and nurture of the Lord, and to the praise of his holy Name. Secondly, it was ordained for a remedy against sin and thirdly, it was ordained for the mutual society, help, and comfort that the one ought to have of the other, both in prosperity and adversity. God Almighty, into which holy estate these two persons present come now to be joined. Therefore if any man can show any just cause, why they may not lawfully be joined together, let him now speak, or else hereafter forever hold his peace."

Her father shifted his feet and cleared his throat and when Hyacinth looked, he was fixing his gaze firmly on the clergyman, making her fight against her smile. Evidently, her father was just as eager for this marriage to take place and was, perhaps, a little frustrated with the time the clergyman was taking to move through these required steps of the ceremony!

"Very well." Again, the clergyman turned his attention to both Hyacinth and Lord Thorne, though to Hyacinth, it seemed like he spoke a little more quickly now. "I require and charge you both, as you will answer at the dreadful day of judgment when the secrets of all hearts shall be disclosed, that if either of you know any impediment why you may not be lawfully joined together in Matrimony, you now confess it. For be you well assured, that so many as are coupled together otherwise than God's Word doth allow are not joined together by God; neither is their Matrimony lawful."

Remaining silent, Hyacinth threw a glance to Lord Thorne, just as he too looked at her. Her heart leaped, a slight tremor in her frame as the time for the vows began. This was the moment when she would make her promises to the Marquess and before God. The time when she would no longer be Lady Hyacinth but instead, the Marchioness of Thorne.

"Lord Thorne?" The clergyman gestured to him. "Will you, Samuel, Marquess of Thorne, take this woman to thy wedded wife, to live together after God's ordinance in the holy estate of Matrimony? Will you love her, comfort her, honor, and keep her in sickness and in health; and, forsaking all other, keep yourself only to her, so long as you both shall live?"

Rather than speaking his words to the clergyman, Lord Thorne turned to look at her as he spoke. "I will."

Her heart exploded in her chest.

"And you, Lady Hyacinth, will you have this man to thy wedded husband, to live together after God's ordinance in the holy estate of Matrimony? Will you obey him, and serve him, love, honor, and keep him in sickness and in health; and, forsaking all others, keep yourself only to him, so long as you both shall live?

She did not hesitate, her fingers burning to touch his. "I will."

The clergyman nodded. "And who is there to give this woman to this man?"

"I am." With a small smile, her father bent to press a kiss to Hyacinth's cheek and, settling her hand on Lord Thorne's arm, stepped back. The heat in Hyacinth's frame did not dissipate as she had expected, but rather it grew, her desire now to be wrapped up in Lord Thorne's arms and held tightly against him.

The clergyman nodded. "Lord Thorne, your vows, if you please."

Turning to face her, Lord Thorne looked down into Hyacinth's eyes, his expression one of tenderness. "I take you as my wedded wife, to have and to hold from this day forward, for better for worse, for richer for poorer, in sickness and in health, to love and to cherish, till death us do part, according to God's holy ordinance."

Hyacinth's throat constricted as joyous tears burned in her eyes. She heard the clergyman speak to her but fought to find her composure, closing her eyes to hide from Lord Thorne for only a moment. "I take you to be my wedded husband, to have and to hold from this day forward, for better for worse, for richer for poorer, in sickness and in health, to love, cherish, and to obey, till death us do part, according to God's holy ordinance."

Her words were only a loud whisper but much to her relief, they appeared to satisfy the clergyman. Opening her eyes, she saw Lord Thorne smiling gently, a lightness in his expression which she knew spoke of love.

"Now we come the giving and receiving of the ring."

It was Lord Elledge's responsibility to hand Lord Thorne the ring, and he did so with a broad smile on his face. His wife, Lady Elledge, was seated in the church and Hyacinth, who had already been introduced, thought her the most wonderful creature and hoped they might soon become close friends.

"Here." Taking her hand, Lord Thorne pushed the ring onto her third finger, shifting just a little closer to her as he did so. "Hyacinth," he murmured, quietly, "with this ring I thee wed. With my body I thee worship, and with all my worldly goods I thee endow."

She could not seem to look away from the ring. It was a symbol, a promise, and a reminder of all that they had shared in these few minutes. She was bound to Lord Thorne now, and he to her. Her lips lifted gently as happiness tugged her closer to him, his fingers pressing lightly on hers. This truly was the most wonderful moment of her life.

"Finally, we come to the blessing." The clergyman prayed over them both but Hyacinth barely took in a word. All she wanted was to be in Lord Thorne's embrace, to have him hold her close as they whispered their words of love to each other. Her heart was pounding, her breathing quickening as she looked into Lord Thorne's eyes as they whispered an 'Amen', wondering just how long it would be until they were entirely alone.

"Those whom God hath joined together let no man put asunder," the clergyman finished, his voice a little louder now as he addressed the full congregation "In as much as Lord Thorne of Nottingham and Miss Hyacinth Jeffries have consented together in holy wedlock and have witnessed the same before God and this company, and thereto have given and pledged their troth either to other and have declared the same by giving and receiving of a Ring, and by joining of hands; I pronounce that they be Man and Wife together. In the Name of the Father, and of the Son, and of the Holy Ghost. Amen."

I am now his wife. Fresh happiness, such as she had never known before, burst into her heart and poured through her frame, making her tremble. Lord Thorne set one arm about her waist and tugged her lightly against him, though even now, she could not express herself as she wished. It was only when he led her through to the back of the church for the marriage lines that they were finally able to steal a few moments alone.

"It is done." Lord Thorne closed the door to the vestry behind him and, though the clergyman went on ahead, he lingered, keeping Hyacinth between him and the door. "What say you to that, my dear?"

She giggled as he ran one finger lightly down her cheek, feeling as though every part of her was alight. "I can say only good about it, I think."

"You think?" His eyebrows lifted and she laughed softly, only for her laughter to fade as he wrapped both arms about her waist. He did not kiss her, however, seeming to wait for something as he searched her eyes with his own.

"What is it?" Tilting her head a little, she pushed her fingers through his hair by his temple, smiling gently. "You are happy, yes?"

The edge of his lips tipped upwards. "Happy? I am ecstatic! You cannot know the joy that is in my heart at this moment! To have you as my wife is a happiness that I cannot express for it captures every part of me."

Hyacinth stood on her tiptoes and brushed her lips

across his, only for Lord Thorne to let out a low growl and kiss her soundly, sending a curl of heat into her stomach. When they finally broke apart, Hyacinth was forced to catch her breath, another giggle escaping her as she settled one hand against his heart.

"You say the very things that I feel," she told him, speaking a little more softly now, wanting to find the right words to express all that she felt. "I did not ever expect this joy but to know that I am in the arms of a gentleman who loves me as much as I love him brings me such happiness, I can barely believe it."

Lord Thorne smiled and cupped her cheek, leaning closer to her again. "You have captured me completely, Hyacinth. It is because of you that we have found this happiness, because of you that we are stepping forward into a future together." His thumb brushed lightly across her skin. "I love you with all of my heart, and I swear to you that I always shall."

Hyacinth and Lord Thorne turned out to be a perfect match!

This is the last book in the Whispers of the Ton series. Have you read the first book in the Only for Love series? The Wallflower's Unseen Charm

Read ahead for a sneak peek!

MY DEAR READER

Thank you for reading and supporting my books! I hope this story brought you some escape from the real world into the always captivating Regency world. A good story, especially one with a happy ending, just brightens your day and makes you feel good! If you enjoyed the book, would you leave a review on Amazon? Reviews are always appreciated.

Below is a complete list of all my books! Why not click and see if one of them can keep you entertained for a few hours?

The Duke's Daughters Series
The Duke's Daughters: A Sweet Regency Romance Boxset
A Rogue for a Lady
My Restless Earl
Rescued by an Earl
In the Arms of an Earl
The Reluctant Marquess (Prequel)

A Smithfield Market Regency Romance
The Smithfield Market Romances: A Sweet Regency Romance Boxset
The Rogue's Flower
Saved by the Scoundrel
Mending the Duke
The Baron's Malady

The Returned Lords of Grosvenor Square
The Returned Lords of Grosvenor Square: A Regency Romance Boxset
The Waiting Bride
The Long Return
The Duke's Saving Grace
A New Home for the Duke

The Spinsters Guild
The Spinsters Guild: A Sweet Regency Romance Boxset
A New Beginning
The Disgraced Bride
A Gentleman's Revenge
A Foolish Wager
A Lord Undone

Convenient Arrangements
Convenient Arrangements: A Regency Romance Collection
A Broken Betrothal
In Search of Love
Wed in Disgrace
Betrayal and Lies
A Past to Forget
Engaged to a Friend

Landon House
Landon House: A Regency Romance Boxset
Mistaken for a Rake
A Selfish Heart
A Love Unbroken
A Christmas Match
A Most Suitable Bride

An Expectation of Love

Second Chance Regency Romance
Second Chance Regency Romance Boxset
Loving the Scarred Soldier
Second Chance for Love
A Family of her Own
A Spinster No More

Soldiers and Sweethearts
Soldiers and Sweethearts Boxset
To Trust a Viscount
Whispers of the Heart
Dare to Love a Marquess
Healing the Earl
A Lady's Brave Heart

Ladies on their Own: Governesses and Companions
Ladies on their Own Boxset
More Than a Companion
The Hidden Governess
The Companion and the Earl
More than a Governess
Protected by the Companion

Lost Fortunes, Found Love
Lost Fortunes, Found Love Boxset
A Viscount's Stolen Fortune
For Richer, For Poorer
Her Heart's Choice
A Dreadful Secret
Their Forgotten Love
His Convenient Match

Only for Love
Only for Love : A Clean Regency Boxset
The Heart of a Gentleman
A Lord or a Liar
The Earl's Unspoken Love
The Viscount's Unlikely Ally
The Highwayman's Hidden Heart
Miss Millington's Unexpected Suitor

Waltzing with Wallflowers
The Wallflower's Unseen Charm
The Wallflower's Midnight Waltz
Wallflower Whispers
The Ungainly Wallflower
The Determined Wallflower
The Wallflower's Secret (Revenge of the Wallflowers series)
The Wallflower's Choice

Whispers of the Ton
The Truth about the Earl
The Truth about the Rogue
The Truth about the Marquess
The Truth about the Viscount
The Truth about the Duke
The Truth about the Lady

Christmas in London Series
The Uncatchable Earl
The Undesirable Duke

Christmas Kisses Series
Christmas Kisses Box Set
The Lady's Christmas Kiss

The Viscount's Christmas Queen
Her Christmas Duke

Christmas Stories
Love and Christmas Wishes: Three Regency Romance Novellas
A Family for Christmas
Mistletoe Magic: A Regency Romance
Heart, Homes & Holidays: A Sweet Romance Anthology

Happy Reading!
All my love,
Rose

A SNEAK PEEK OF THE WALLFLOWER'S UNSEEN CHARM

PROLOGUE

"You must promise me that you will *try*."

Miss Joy Bosworth rolled her eyes at her mother.

"Try to be more like my elder sisters, yes? That *is* what you mean, is it not?"

"And what is wrong with being like them?" Lady Halifax's stern tone told Joy in no uncertain terms that to criticize Bettina, Sarah, and Mary – all three of whom had married within the last few years – was a very poor decision indeed. Wincing, Joy fell silent and dropped her gaze to her lap as her beleaguered lady's maid continued to fix her hair. This was the third time that her lady's maid had set her hair, for the first two attempts had been deemed entirely unsuitable by Joy's mother – though quite what was wrong with it, Joy had been completely unable to see.

"You are much too forward, too quick to give your opinion," her mother continued, gazing at Joy's reflection in the looking glass, her eyes narrowing a little. "All of your elder sisters are quiet, though Bettina perhaps a little too much so, but their husbands greatly appreciate that about them!

They speak when they are asked to speak, give their opinion when it is desired and otherwise say very little when it comes to matters which do not concern them. *You,* on the other hand, speak when you are *not* asked to do so, give your opinion most readily, and say a great deal on *any* subject even when it does not concern you!"

Hearing the strong emphasis, Joy chose not to drop her head further, as her mother might have expected, but instead to lift her chin and look back steadily. She was not about to be cowed when it came to such a trait. In some ways, she was rather proud of her determination to speak as she thought, for she was the only one of her sisters who did so. Mayhap it was simply because she was the youngest, but Joy did not truly know why - she had always been determined to speak up for herself and, simply because she was in London, was not, she thought, cause to alter herself now!

"You must find a suitable husband!" Exclaiming aloud, Lady Halifax threw up her hands, perhaps seeing the glint of steel in Joy's eyes. "Continuing to behave as you are will not attract anyone to you, I can assure you of that!"

"The *right* gentleman would still be attracted," Joy shot back, adding her own emphasis. "There must be some amongst society who do not feel the same way as you, Mother. I do not seek to disagree with you, only to suggest that there might be a little more consideration in some, or even a different viewpoint altogether!"

"I know what I am talking about!" Lady Halifax smote Joy gently on the shoulder though her expression was one of frustration. "I have already had three daughters wed and it would do you well to listen to me and my advice."

Joy did not know what to say. Yes, she had listened to her mother on many an occasion, but that did not mean that she had to take everything her mother said to heart... and on this occasion, she was certain that Lady Halifax was quite wrong.

"If I am not true to who I am, Mama, then will that not make for a very difficult marriage?"

"A difficult marriage?" This was said with such a degree of astonishment that Joy could not help but smile. "There is no such thing as a difficult marriage, not unless one of the two parties *within* the marriage itself attempts to make it so. Do you not understand, Joy? I am telling you to alter yourself so that you do *not* cause any difficulties, both for yourself now, and for your husband in the future."

The smile on Joy's face slipped and then blew away, her forehead furrowing as she looked at her mother again. Lady Halifax was everything a lady of quality ought to be, and she had trained each of her daughters to be as she was… except that Joy had never been the success her other daughters had been. Even now, the thought of stepping into marriage with a gentleman she barely knew, simply because he was deemed suitable, was rather horrifying to Joy, and was made all the worse by the idea that she would somehow have to pretend to be someone she was not!

"As I have said, Joy, you will try."

This time, Joy realized, it was not a question her mother had been asking her but a statement. A statement which said that she was expected to do nothing other than what her mother said – and to do so without question also.

I shall not lie.

"I think my hair is quite presentable now, Mama." Steadfastly refusing to either agree with or refuse what her mother had said, Joy sat up straight in her chair, her head lifting, her shoulders dropping low as she turned her head from side to side. "Very elegant, I must say."

"The ribbon is not the right color."

Joy resisted the urge to roll her eyes for what would be the second time.

"Mama, it is a light shade of green and it is threaded through the many braids Clara has tied my hair into. It is quite perfect and cannot be faulted. Besides, it does match the gown perfectly. You made certain of that yourself."

So saying, she threw a quick smile to her lady's maid and saw a twitch of Clara's lips before the maid bowed her head, stepping back so that Lady Halifax would not see the smile on her face.

"It is not quite as I would want it, but it will have to do." Lady Halifax sniffed and waved one hand in Clara's direction. "My daughter requires her gown now. And be quick about it, we are a little short on time."

"If you had not insisted that Clara do my hair on two further occasions, then we would not be in danger of being tardy," Joy remarked, rising from her chair, and walking across the room, quite missing the flash in her mother's eyes. "It was quite suitable the first time."

"*I* shall be the judge of that," came the sharp retort, as Lady Halifax stalked to the door. "Now do hurry up. The carriage is waiting, and I do not want us to bring the attention of the entire *ton* down upon us by walking in much later than any other!"

Joy sighed and nodded, turning back to where Clara was ready with her gown. Coming to London and seeking out a suitable match was not something she could get the least bit excited about, and this ball, rather than being a momentous one, filled with hope and expectation, felt like a heaviness on her shoulders. The sooner it was over, Joy considered, the happier she would be.

CHAPTER ONE

"And Lord Granger is seated there."

"Mm-hm."

Nudging Joy lightly, her mother scowled.

"You are not paying the least bit of attention! Instead, you are much too inclined towards staring! Though quite what you are staring at, I cannot imagine!"

Joy tilted her head but did not take her eyes away from what she had been looking at.

"I was wondering whether that lady there – the one with the rather ornate hairstyle – found it difficult to wear such a thing without difficulty or pain." The lady in question had what appeared to be a bird's nest of some description, adorned with feathers and lace, planted on one side of her head, with her hair going through it as though it were a part of the creation. There was also a bird sitting on the edge of the nest, though to Joy's eyes, it looked rather monstrous and not at all as it ought. "Surely it must be stuck to her head in some way." She could not keep a giggle back when the lady curtsied and then rose, only for her magnificent headpiece to wobble terribly. "Oh dear, perhaps it is not as well secured as it ought to be!"

"Will you stop speaking so loudly?"

The hiss from Lady Halifax had Joy's attention snapping back to her mother, a slight flush touching the edge of her cheeks as she realized that one or two of the other ladies near them were glancing in her direction. She had spoken a little too loudly for both her own good and her mother's liking.

"My apologies, Mama."

"I should think so!" Lady Halifax grabbed Joy's arm in a somewhat tight grip and then began to walk in the opposite direction of that taken by the lady with the magnificent hair. "Pray do not embarrass both me and yourself, with your hasty tongue!"

"I do not mean to," Joy muttered, allowing her mother to take her in whatever direction she wished. "I simply speak as I think."

"A trait I ought to have worked out of you by now, but instead, it seems determined to cling to you!" With a sigh, Lady Halifax shook her head. "Now look, do you see there?"

Coming to a hasty stop, Joy looked across the room, following the direction of her mother's gaze. "What is it that you wish me to look at, Mama?"

"Those young ladies there," came the reply. "Do you see them? They stand clustered together, hidden in the shadows of the ballroom. Even their own mothers or sponsors have given up on them!"

A frown tugged at Joy's forehead.

"I do not know what you are speaking of Mama."

"The wallflowers!" Lady Halifax turned sharply to Joy, her eyes flashing. "Do you not see them? They stand there, doing nothing other than adorning the wall. They are passed over constantly, ignored by the gentlemen of the *ton,* who care very little for their company."

"Then that is the fault of the gentlemen of the *ton*," Joy answered, a little upset by her mother's remarks. "I do not think it is right to blame the young ladies for such a thing."

Lady Halifax groaned aloud, closing her eyes.

"Why do you willfully misunderstand? They are not wallflowers by choice, but because they are deemed as unsuitable for marriage, for one reason or another."

"Which, again, might not be their own doing."

"Perhaps, but all the same," Lady Halifax continued, sounding more exasperated than ever, "I have shown you these young ladies as a warning."

Joy's eyebrows shot towards her hairline.

"A warning?"

"Yes, that you will yourself become one such young lady if you do not begin to behave yourself and act as you ought." Moving so that she faced Joy directly, Lady Halifax narrowed her eyes a little. "You will find yourself standing there with them, doing nothing other than watching the gentlemen of London take various *other* young ladies out to dance, rather than showing any genuine interest in you. Would that not be painful? Would that not trouble you?"

The answer her mother wished her to give was evident to Joy, but she could not bring herself to say it. It was not that she wanted to cause her mother any pain, but that she could not permit herself to be false, not even if it would bring her a little comfort.

"It might," she admitted, eventually, as Lady Halifax let out another stifled groan, clearly exasperated. "But as I have said before, Mama, I do not wish to be courted by a gentleman who is unaware of my true nature. I do not see why I should hide myself away, simply so that I can please a suitor. If such a thing were to happen, if I were to be willing to act in that way, it would not make for a happy arrangement. Sooner or later, my real self would return to the fore, and then what would my husband do? It is not as though he could step back from our marriage. Therefore, I would be condemning both him and myself, to a life of misery. I do not think that would be at all agreeable."

"That is where you are wrong." Lady Halifax lifted her chin, though she looked straight ahead. "To be wed is the most satisfactory situation one can find oneself in, regardless of the circumstances. It is not as though you will spend a great deal of time with your husband so, therefore, you will never need to reveal your 'true nature', as you put it."

The more her mother talked, the more Joy found herself growing almost despondent, such was the picture Lady Halifax was painting of what would be waiting for her. She understood that yes, she was here to find a suitable match, but to then remove to her husband's estate, where she would spend most of her days alone and only be in her husband's company whenever he desired it, did not seem to Joy to be a very pleasant circumstance. That would be very dull indeed, would it not? Her existence would become small, insignificant, and utterly banal, and that was certainly *not* the future Joy wanted for herself.

"Now, do lift your head up, stand tall, and smile," came the command. "We must go and speak to Lord Falconer and Lord Dartford at once."

Joy hid her sigh by lowering her head, her eyes squeezing closed for a few moments. There was no time to protest, however, no time to explain to her mother that what had just been discussed had settled Joy's mind against such things as this, for Lady Halifax once more marched Joy across the room and, before she knew it, introduced Joy to the two gentlemen whom she had pointed out, as well as to one Lady Dartford, who was Lord Dartford's mother.

"Good evening." Joy rose from her curtsey and tried to smile, though her smile was a little lackluster. "How very glad I am to make your acquaintance."

"Said quite perfectly." Lord Dartford chuckled, his dark eyes sweeping across her features, then dropping down to her frame as Joy blushed furiously. "So, you are next in line to try your hand at the marriage mart?"

"Next in line?"

"Yes." Lord Dartford waved a hand as though to dismiss her words and her irritation, which Joy had attempted to make more than evident by the sweep of her eyebrow. "You have three elder sisters do you not?"

"Yes, I do." Joy kept her eyebrows lifted. "All of whom are all now wed and settled."

"And now you must do the same." Lord Dartford chuckled, but Joy did not smile. The sound was not a pleasant one. "Unfortunately, none of your sisters were able to catch my eye and, alas, I do not think that you will be able to do so either."

"Dartford!"

His mother's gasp of horror was clear, but Joy merely smiled, her stomach twisting at the sheer arrogance which the gentleman had displayed.

"That is a little forward of you, Lord Dartford," she remarked, speaking quite clearly, and ignoring the way that her mother set one hand to the small of her back in clear warning. "What is to say that I would have any interest in *your* company?"

This response wiped the smile from Lord Dartford's face. His dark eyes narrowed, and his jaw set but, much to

Joy's delight, his friend began to guffaw, slapping Lord Dartford on the shoulder.

"You have certainly been set in your place!" Lord Falconer laughed as Joy looked back into Lord Dartford's angry expression without flinching. "And the lady is quite right, that was one of the most superior things I have heard you say this evening!"

"Only this evening?" Enjoying herself far too much, Joy tilted her head and let a smile dance across her features. "Again, Lord Dartford, I ask you what difference it would make to me to have a gentleman such as yourself interested in furthering their acquaintance with me? It is not as though I must simply accept every gentleman who comes to seek me out, is it? And I can assure you, I certainly would not accept you!"

Lord Falconer laughed again but Lord Dartford's eyes narrowed all the more, his jaw tight and his frame stiff with clear anger and frustration.

"I do not think a young lady such as yourself should display such audacity, Miss Bosworth."

"And if I want your opinion, Lord Dartford, then I will ask you for it," Joy shot back, just as quickly. "Thus far, I do not recall doing so."

"We must excuse ourselves."

The hand that had been on Joy's back now turned into a pressing force that propelled her away from Lord Dartford, Lord Falconer, and Lady Dartford – the latter of whom was standing, staring at Joy with wide eyes, her face a little pale.

"Do excuse us."

Lady Halifax inclined her head and then took Joy's hand, grasping it tightly rather than with any gentleness whatsoever, dragging her away from the gentlemen she had only just introduced Joy to.

"Mama, you are hurting me!" Pulling her hand away, Joy scowled when her mother rounded on her. "Please, you must stop–"

"Do you know what you have done?"

The hissed words from her mother had Joy stopping short, a little surprised at her mother's vehemence.

"I have done nothing other than speak my mind and set Lord Dartford – someone who purports to be a gentleman – back into his place. I do not know what makes him think that I would have *any* interest in–"

"News of this will spread through London!" Lady Halifax blinked furiously, and it was only then that Joy saw the tears in her mother's eyes. "This is your very first ball on the eve of your come out, and you decide to speak with such force and impudence to the Earl of Dartford?"

A writhing began to roll itself around Joy's stomach.

"I do not know what you mean. I did nothing wrong."

"It is not about wrong or right," came the reply, as Lady Halifax whispered with force towards Joy. "It is about wisdom. You did not speak with any wisdom this evening, and now news of what you did will spread throughout society. Lady Dartford will see to that."

Joy lifted her shoulders and then let them fall.

"I could not permit Lord Dartford to speak to me in such a way. I am worthy of respect, am I not?"

"You could have ignored him!" Lady Halifax threw up her hands, no longer managing to maintain her composure, garnering the attention of one or two others nearby. "You did not have to say a single thing! A simple look – or a slight curl of the lip – would have sufficed. Instead, you did precisely what I told you not to do and now news of your audacity will spread through London. Lady Dartford is one of the most prolific gossips in all of London and given that you insulted her son, I fear for what she will say."

Joy kept her chin lifted.

"Mama, Lady Dartford was shocked at her own son's remarks to me."

"But that does not mean that she will speak of *him* in the same way that she will speak of you," Lady Halifax told her, a single tear falling as red spots appeared on her cheeks. "Do you not understand, Joy?"

"Lord Falconer laughed at what I said."

Lady Halifax closed her eyes.

"That means nothing, other than the fact that he found your remarks and your behavior to be mirthful. It will not save your reputation."

"I did nothing to ruin my reputation."

"Oh, but you did." A flash came into her mother's eyes. "You may not see it as yet, but I can assure you, you have done yourself a great deal of damage. I warned you, I *asked* you to be cautious and instead, you did the opposite. Now, within the first ball of the Season, your sharp tongue and your determination to speak as you please has brought you into greater difficulty than you can imagine." Her eyes closed, a heavy sigh breaking from her. "Mayhap you will become a wallflower after all."

Hmm, my mother always said my mouth would get me into trouble...and now Miss Bosworth could be in trouble! Check out the rest of the story on the Kindle store The Wallflower's Unseen Charm

JOIN MY MAILING LIST AND FACEBOOK READER GROUP

Sign up for my newsletter to stay up to date on new releases, contests, giveaways, freebies, and deals!

Free book with signup!

Monthly Facebook Giveaways! Books and Amazon gift cards!
Join my reader group on Facebook!

Rose's Ravenous Readers

Facebook Page: https://www.facebook.com/rosepearsonauthor

Website: www.RosePearsonAuthor.com
You can sign up for my Newsletter on my website too!

Follow me on Goodreads: Author Page